CURSED

Andréa Joy

Cursed
The Fallen Duet 1

ISBN: 978-1-9992413-3-9

Cover Design by: Raven Designs

Editied by: Nikki Holt Sexton

Proof read by: Sarah Strawinski

Formatting by: Andrea Joy

AUTHOR NOTE

Even though this story takes place in Toronto, Canada, the author has taken some creative liberties with locations, street names, and buildings within the book.

DEDICATION

To Nicole and Maddy, you're in our thoughts and prayers. We love you.

CHAPTER ONE

ARLO

QUEEN'S UNIVERSITY

I stare up at the Victorian style structure. A nervous excitement courses through me making my stomach roll. This is what four years of hard work and barely any social life has amounted to. If you ask me why, out of all the universities and colleges in Toronto,

Ontario had I picked Queens. I wouldn't know what to tell you, except that I saw a picture of the school in a newspaper article when I was a kid and instantly knew that this was where I wanted to go. Even at a young age I felt an unexplainable pull to this school. The red brick buildings called to me like nothing I could ever remember. It looked so grand in the picture, like somewhere the Royal Family would've attended, and I wanted to be a part of that.

I used to make up these games, where I would pretend that I was part of the Royal Family. That Princess Diana was my mother. Not that my own was evil or anything. I actually think I have the best mom any kid would be lucky to have, but I dreamt about the extravagance of it all. The big four poster bed, a pool, and a big back yard. We didn't have much while I was growing up. Mom worked her ass off to provide for us, but some months were still harder than others ever since my dad passed away. He was an officer in the Royal Canadian Navy, and one day he just never came home after being deployed. I was six. I only got up the courage to ask my mom one time, ten years later, what had happened to him but she had clammed up and changed the subject. At the time, I thought it was weird. But, I was also a teenager, so a few minutes later I had already moved on to the next major problem I was facing; the upcoming biology final. I never asked her about my dad again and she hasn't volunteered any information in the three years since.

The hallways are crowded when I finally manage to get my feet moving and ascend the stairs up from the sidewalk. There's people everywhere. Some on their way to their first class of the day, others just standing around catching up after the summer. I stop just inside the double wooden doors and gawk. I'm definitely not in Oshawa anymore. Not that my home town is small, well, I guess compared to this it can be considered small town. But holy shit, there's a lot of people here.

Someone bumps into my arm making me jolt and I quickly turn to apologize but no words come out when I catch a glimpse of the man walking by me. He's gorgeous. His inky black hair is a little on the long side, causing his bangs to slip into his eyes. When he rakes a hand through them to push them back, I want to sigh dreamily. His eyes are as bright as the turquoise Mediterranean Sea and I equal parts want to feel them trained on me and want to hide from their intensity. He smirks when he sees me standing there and then three other sets of eyes turn my way, each more intense than the other.

"Hey, move it!" A frustrated voice says from behind me and just like that, the spell from the four guys is broken.

"Sorry." Hiking the strap of my back-pack up higher on my shoulder, I glance at my phone again and see that I only have ten minutes before my first class starts. I pull up the campus map and search for the right building. Realizing that it's all the way across campus, I start moving, almost speed walking. I hate being late. I especially hate being late to my first class at a new school. Regardless of the fact that I'm not the only freshman.

Thankfully, I make it to WRLD 310R: Mythologies in Motion before the professor and find a seat near the back. Since it's the first class, I tend to start the semester at the back of the class and slowly make my towards the front as the semester progresses and I get more comfortable with the class. Usually, third year classes are restricted to those in their third or fourth year, but when I found out this was the last year this class was going to be offered, I emailed the prof and got special permission to take it despite only being a first year. I guess my grade 12 English grades were good enough for her to agree.

I've just sat down and pulled out my brand-new laptop when the door opens again and the four guys from earlier stroll in. Almost immediately, the atmosphere in the room shifts. Conversations stop as everyone waits. For what? I don't know.

The one with the turquoise eyes, laughs at something one of the other guys says and when he looks up and those eyes connect with mine, I stop breathing. He winks and then the four of them take up seats on the other side of the lecture hall, but in the same row as me.

"Welcome to Mythologies in Motion. I am your professor for this course, Mackenzie Porter. But you can call me Mac."

My attention is pulled away from the four guys to the front of the class when the prof begins the introductory lesson. When I first came across this course while I was picking out my classes on the school's student services website I was intrigued. I've always found mythologies and conspiracy theories interesting, but my high school classes never really tackled the subjects. Not that one has anything to do with the other, that's just where I found the majority of my interests being pulled.

The first class goes by quick with Mac just going over what we can expect out of this course for the semester. From the grading outline, and what mythologies we'll be touching on. Before I know it, the hour and twenty minutes is up and everyone is packing up and leaving to head toward their next class. The hairs on the back of my neck prickle as I swing my backpack over my shoulder and descend the stairs back down to the front of the class. When I look back, I find all four guys watching me.

CHAPTER TWO

ARLO

COMPARED TO MY first class, the next one is a little boring. Being a freshman means having to take the boring pre-req classes before you're able to take the real ones that interest you. But that also means taking the courses you hate in order to take the one you really want later on. And that's not including the courses the university makes you take before you can graduate. Personally, I think it's stupid. I'm never going to need Psychology 101 for the career I have in mind. Not unless it has anything to do with marine mammals. My dream job is to photograph marine wildlife. Mainly, Sharks. However, when I broached the subject with my mom shortly after my sixteenth birthday, she made me promise that I would at least get my bachelor's degree first. She said it didn't matter what I majored in, as long as I graduated from university with a degree. I agreed, if she let me take a year off and spend it diving with Sharks off the coast of South Africa. Mom was reluctant, but when she saw that I wasn't going to budge, she gave in. I had to pay for my own way and call her every day, but I was totally okay with that. I was just excited for the opportunity to do what I love.

I get it. I mean, she never had the opportunity to go to post-secondary school when she was younger. Her and my dad had me a few weeks before their high school graduation. They got married soon after and then several months after I was born, dad enlisted and mom was stuck raising an almost one-year old by herself since both sets of grandparents refused to help out. I never had a real relationship with my grandparents growing up. Not until two years ago when I turned seventeen and they realized that I wasn't going to screw up my life like my parents. Not that I think my parents screwed up their lives, but that was the mentality of my maternal grandparents. Even though they completely ignored me for most of my life, I can't really complain about them now. It's because of them that I'm able to attend one of the best post-secondary schools in the Greater Toronto Area. I never met my paternal grandparents, and I don't remember Dad ever mentioning them before he died.

After my second class lets out, I hit the cafeteria since I have about two hours before my final class of the day starts.

When I was selecting my classes, my goal was to either be done earlier or have classes that started later, cause who doesn't want to be done by one in the afternoon and have the rest of the day to do other stuff or be able to sleep in until noon if they wanted to. Thankfully, I was able to arrange my schedule so that I'll be done with classes by one on Monday, Wednesday and Thursday, and the rest of the week my earliest class is at twelve-thirty. So far, university life isn't half bad.

I grab a BLT wrap and a water from the main cafeteria in the Student Centre. There are other restaurants in this building as well, but all the lines are ridiculously long. Seeing that all the tables are already filled with students, I take my lunch and head back outside and across campus to the quad. I find a shady area across the field from the water fountain and set my bag down before lowering myself to the ground and pulling my knees up. I take a second to look around, still not completely believing that I'm here. I went through a bit of a rebellious phase in grade 9, but when in grade 10 my guidance counsellor told me that I probably wasn't smart enough to get into Queen's University, I had made it my mission to show him that I could. For the next three years I studied my ass off and made honour roll twice. When I opened that acceptance letter, I cried. I mean, I won't say that there wasn't a doubt in my mind that I would get in because there was. His words kept playing on a loop in my head every time I doubted myself over those three years and then to finally have the proof that my hard work had paid off was indescribable. But I did it, and I'm here. *Ha! Look at me now asshole!* But seriously, who says shit like that to a fifteen-year-old?

I finish my wrap and lean my head back against the tree at my back, closing my eyes and taking in the sun on my skin and the sounds of the campus around me. That is until sounds of a scuffle nearby draws my attention. On the other side of the field, some guy in a rugby jersey is facing off with one of the four guys from my mythologies class. He's wearing a leather jacket in the September humid weather, motorcycle helmet clenched tightly in his grip at his side. When rugby jersey shoves at his chest, he drops the helmet and that's when the doors to the gym fly open and the other three guys race out. Turquoise eyes immediately steps between the two. I can't hear what they're saying but I'm assuming he's telling rugby jersey to take a hike. At first it looks like he's going to refuse but then thinks better of it when all four guys cross their arms and stare him down, their stance obviously brokering no argument.

"Those are the Four Horsemen," a voice says from beside me.

I startle, nearly jumping fifty feet in the air and have to press a hand to my chest to keep my heart from beating out of it.

The girl giggles, her purple hair gleaming in the sun shining through the leaves of the tree overhead. "Sorry. I thought you knew I was here. I'm Julie," she says.

"Arlo, and that's okay. I was kinda in my own world."

The corner of her thin lips pulls up and she scrunches her nose in confusion. "Arlo? Is that short for something? If not, that's cool. I like it."

I chuckle and tuck a piece of my chocolate brown hair back behind my ear. "It's short for Charlotte. I've been Arlo all my life that Charlotte just sounds weird, you know?" I shrug, not sure why I'm telling all this to a stranger.

"Cool." She digs around in her purse before pulling out a small Tupperware container. "Pot brownie?" she asks, tilting it so I can see inside. I chew on my bottom lip not really sure how to refuse them without seeming like a bitch or stuck up. I have nothing against pot. It's legal in Canada now, but I've just never had any experience with it. My gaze shoots up to Julie's blue ones when she laughs. "You should see your face. I was kidding. They're just regular brownies. But if you'd prefer the pot ones, I have those too." She grins. I return it and warily take one square of the baked good.

"When you said they're the four horsemen, what did you mean by that?" I ask, my gaze darting back over to the four guys who are now talking to an older gentleman in a suit.

"That's the Dean," Julie says, following my line of sight. "War, Famine, Plague, and Death. The Four Horsemen of the Apocalypse."

"As in the New Testament?"

Julie nods, taking a bite out of her brownie. When she's done, she continues, "I have no idea where the nickname came from, but that's how they're known to everyone around here." She rolls her eyes. "It's dumb if you ask me."

Julie and I talk for a bit. I find out that she's actually a third-year business student. I'm ashamed to admit that I'm shocked. I never would've pegged her for being into business with the purple hair and boho outfit, but she laughs off my shock with a wave of her hand. After a while, we go back to watching the four guys talk to the Dean of the university for a few minutes until the older man turns and storms off leaving the four younger ones looking pissed off. One of them says something to the group and they all nod before leather jacket picks up his helmet from the ground and they leave together as a group.

"How do you know them?" I ask, figuring the question's stupid and she'll tell me that it's common knowledge. So, I'm surprised when she shrugs again, stuffing the Tupperware back into her purse and stands before offering me a hand up.

"Kane's my step brother," she says, like I'm supposed to know who that is. "C'mon, I'll show you around."

CHAPTER THREE

HUNTER

"BURGESS IS STARTING to piss me off," Kane grits out, throwing a right hook at the punching bag. "Who the hell does he think he is."

Jagger snorts from the other side of the bag. "I'm sure if you didn't insist on picking a fight with every asshole who doesn't like you, he'd leave you alone."

Kane growls, throwing another punch and sending the bag swinging hard into Jagger.

"Oy! Watch it, asshole!" Jagger grumbles and Kane smirks.

"So," Wolf says, throwing himself down on the couch beside me and kicking his feet up onto the coffee table. "Do you think it's her?"

Silence descends around the room as all three of my best friends look to me. Images of the new girl flood my head. The deer in headlights look she gave me when I accidentally bumped into her this morning. Her grey eyes wide and innocent looked so odd against the dark brown hair falling down her back in loose curls. I drain the rest of my beer and place the bottle on the table beside Wolf's feet before pushing up and walking over to the pool table in the corner of the living room. The four of us moved into this house freshman year and over the years it's been known as the place to be for students on Friday nights.

"I don't know," I reply, picking up a cue. An hour and twenty-minute class wasn't enough time to determine who the freshman in our third-year world literature class is beyond her name.

"She looks like him," Kane says, discarding his boxing gloves on a workout bench nearby and grabbing a sweat towel.

"That's not enough," Wolf counters, getting up from the couch and coming over to pick up another pool cue.

I rack the balls and then Wolf and I rock-paper-scissors to see who goes first. Wolf wins and the first ball he sinks is a stripe.

"We'll keep an eye on her," I say, lining up my shot when it's my turn and sinking a solid. "But for now, we keep this to ourselves. The Elders don't need to know about her yet."

The guys mutter their agreement and Wolf and I go back and forth until I sink the last solid as well as the eight-ball. Wolf curses but gets out his wallet anyway and hands me a crisp one-hundred-dollar bill.

"One of these days, someone's going to hand you your ass," he grumbles, flipping me off.

"Not likely."

We spend the rest of the night bullshitting and talking about the classes we all have this semester, but my head just isn't in it. I can't help thinking about her. Charlotte Williams. If she is who we think she is then this year just got a whole lot more interesting, and I'm not entirely sure that's a good thing.

CHAPTER FOUR

ARLO

"HOW WAS YOUR first week?" Mom asks when I finally get a chance to call her on Thursday evening.

"It was good. Different. It seemed like this week was mostly just easing us into the new semester so we'll see how next week goes," I answer, holding the phone between my cheek and shoulder while I try to drain the water from the pot. Once I'm satisfied I got all the water out, I place the pot back on the stove and remove the lid before reaching for the jar of spaghetti sauce. I admit it's not the healthiest dinner, but I haven't had a chance to do a decent grocery shop yet. I'm hoping to change that this weekend.

Along with paying my tuition, my grandparents surprised me with a condo off campus. It's far enough away from the school that I don't feel like I'm constantly at school but close enough that I can walk and not have to take the TTC. Mom was angry when she found out about the tuition and the condo. I know she feels guilty that she couldn't offer to help me pay my tuition herself and I felt bad for accepting the money from the grandparents who originally wanted nothing to do with my family, but university tuition is fucking expensive. I didn't want to accept it, but I also didn't want to be drowning in student loan payments for years after graduation either. I know that eventually the money will come with some stipulation or other but I'm willing to do whatever they ask if it means I get to graduate with a degree from the university I've always dreamt about.

Mom and I talk for another few minutes. She tells me about this guy she met at the grocery store who asked her out on a date. I'm happy for her. She hasn't had anyone in her life since dad.

"Are you going to go?" I ask, stacking my bowl in the dishwasher and putting the leftover spaghetti in the fridge.

"I don't know, Charlotte. I haven't been on a date since your dad." The tone in her voice changes and I know she's remembering a time from long ago when he was still alive. It doesn't sound as sad as it did years ago, but I can tell she still misses him.

"Well, you should. And if you don't like him then at least you got a free meal out of it," I tease, trying to lighten the mood. Our relationship has always been that of a friendship than a mother/daughter.

I think that just came from mom being a kid herself when she had me.

She laughs. “Maybe I will. Will you be home for lunch on Sunday?”

“I wouldn’t miss it. The Go Train gets into Oshawa at eleven.”

Mom says she’ll pick me up then. We say goodbye and I hang up, feeling a little better now that I’ve talked to her. This is the first time that we’ve been a part for so long. Even when I used to go camping with the one friend I had in high school, it was only for the weekend. I roll my eyes at myself and pick up the tv remote. I’m such a momma’s girl. I absently flip through the channels until a show catches my attention. My phone pings with a message.

Julie: Get dressed. We’re going out. Party at the docks.

After that day under the tree, Julie and I became fast friends. We exchanged numbers after she gave me a more detailed tour of the campus – nothing like the guided tour I did before I applied for admission – and we’ve met for lunch whenever we both have breaks between classes. This, though, will be the first time we've hung out off campus.

Me: Can't I already have an assignment due next week.

Julie: *snore* C'mon, Arlo, live a little. You have the entire weekend to do homework.

I chew on my bottom lip while weighing the pros and cons. It would be fun to go out again. To reconnect with the person I was, before getting into university took over my life. I lost a lot of friends in those three years from cancelling plans and preferring to study than attend bush parties or whatever party was happening that weekend. Plus, I think I deserve a night out. If nothing than to celebrate the fact that I'm at my dream school.

When I don't text back right away, another message from Julie comes through.

Julie: My brother and his friends will be there.

I may have failed to keep my curiosity about the four guys a secret over the last week. Not like it would've been hard to guess. Every time one of them entered the room my attention would immediately be drawn to them. And if all four of them were together? Pfft, forget it. I couldn't concentrate worth shit. Which made WRLD both interesting and frustrating. Especially because they kept sitting in the same row as me and more than once I've caught at least one of them staring at me.

I text Julie back, "okay, fine." Then go about pulling every single item of clothing I own from my closet and throwing them onto my bed so that I can pick an outfit.

I'm still staring at the three outfits I've narrowed it down to when there's a knock on my bedroom door. Julie pokes her head in first before pushing the door open all the way to step inside.

"Your roommate let me in," she says by explanation, coming to stand beside me. She eyes the outfits I have sprawled out and then picks up a black spaghetti strap body suit I had paired with leggings and dark skinny jeans I had paired with a flowy top. She shoves both items into my chest. I clutch them in my arms, stunned, as she fingers my hair and hums. "I like the messy wave look you got going on. I think I can work with this. Now, go get changed and we'll do your makeup."

I raise a brow at her commanding tone. "Hi Julie. How are you? Me? I'm well, thank you."

She snorts but tilts her head and stares like she's waiting for something.

"What?" I ask.

"Get changed. We don't have a lot of time."

"What? Here?" I squeak, causing her to roll her eyes.

"You don't have anything I haven't seen before, babe. But also," she hooks a thumb over her shoulder, "you do have a perfectly good bathroom if you're uncomfortable changing in front of someone."

I hurry out to the shared bathroom down the hall and get changed before going back to my room so Julie can do my hair and makeup. Twenty minutes later, we're piling into Julie's car and driving to the party.

She pulls her car into a parking lot at the docks in the Warehouse District. If it weren't for the throes of people spilling out into the parking lot and onto the docks, and the loud thump of bass I would think we were in the wrong place.

"Are we allowed to be here?" I ask, following Julie around the front of the car and over to the building that is the source of the loud music.

"Probably not," she answers with a slight lift of her shoulders. "But it's fine."

She leads us through the open doors and over to where someone has set up a makeshift bar. She hands me a can of Bud Light and I absentmindedly grab it while my eyes roam around the building, taking in the massive amounts of people. All students from the looks of it. The warehouse has been completely emptied, and it's not like some of those with two stories, it's just one giant room with a cement floor and metal walls. A DJ booth is set up across the room from the bar and there's a makeshift dance floor between them. Couples grind against each other to the beat of the music.

We're not here long before Julie's attention is already captured by a guy who just walked in. I leave them alone to talk and wander around the open space and then outside when it gets to be a little too hot in the building. The breeze coming off the water is nice and I stop for a second to breathe in the fresh air with my eyes closed.

"Enjoying the party?" A deep voice says from behind me, making me jump.

Beer spills over the side of the can and over my fingers as I swing around. One of the Four Horsemen grins back at me, his head cocked to the side while his eyes trace over my face like I'm a puzzle he's trying to figure out. It's too dark to make out his features, but I can tell that his hair is dark; short on the sides and a little longer on the top with some of it falling into his eyes. He's tall. Taller than me by at least a foot. And the leather jacket and biker boots make him look like a badass. I can't tell if he's the same one from the field earlier in the week with the motorcycle helmet, though, because I can't see his face in the dark. Hell, for all I know they could all own motorcycles. *God, that's hot.* I can just picture sitting on the back of one of their bikes, my body wrapped around one of theirs as the bike vibrates between my thighs. I shiver but play it off as being cold.

"I…" I clear my throat and try again. "I am." I lift my beer, like the very fact that I'm holding a drink is proof enough of how much fun I'm having. I roll my eyes at myself. *Smooth, Arlo.*

"You're in World 310 with Mac," he says, still staring at me in that way that makes me think he sees more than I'd like.

I try not to shift my weight from foot to foot and instead slide the tips of my fingers into the front pockets of my jeans. "I am."

He hums like he's trying to figure out a complicated problem. I want to ask him what his name is. In fact, it's on the tip of my tongue when someone yells from out on the dock.

"Yo, Wolf. Kane's at it again."

Another one of the four joins us. His gaze ping pongs between me and who I now know is Wolf. A slow grin curls the corners of his lips but then it disappears as fast as it appeared when the newcomer looks back at Wolf.

"We gotta go before he kills someone this time," the newcomer says, making Wolf curse.

"'Cuse me," he says to me before the two of them begin pushing through the crowd that's gathered in the middle of the parking lot.

My curiosity getting the better of me, I begin pushing my way through the crowd as well. When I've managed to push my way to the front, two guys are facing off in a makeshift ring. Their shirts off and their hands up in a fighting stance. I instantly recognize one of them as one of the Four Horsemen. I'm assuming he's Kane. His hair is buzzed short to the scalp. Tattoos I hadn't seen earlier adorn both his arms and the left side of his neck. His lips are moving in what I can only assume is a taunt at the other guy because the crowd around us are so loud in their cheering it's hard to hear what is said between the two men.

The other guy throws the first punch and it's over before it even begins. Kane hits him with a one, two combination and a kick causing him to fly back, knocking him out. All around me, money exchanges hands and Hunter, Wolf, and the other Horseman step in the middle to high-five Kane. The nameless one says something and tips his head to the side. Kane gives him a clipped nod and then one by one they slip from the group seemingly undetected.

Just as I'm about to turn around and go in search of Julie, I pause when I overhear a conversation between a group of girls from my Mythologies class.

"Did you hear what that they did to that guy who got up in Kane's face last week?"

"No," one of the girls whispers. In my periphery I see two girls lean in closer to hear what the third girl has to say. "What?"

'They broke both of his arms and his leg. Poor guy will probably have to relearn how to walk."

Their jaws drop and their eyes bug out simultaneously. If I wasn't so curious about what they were talking about I would laugh.

After several seconds, one of them recovers enough to say, "they're all monsters."

"But they're fucking hot monsters," one of them chimes in and they all nod in agreement while staring at something across the way. I follow their gaze and lock eyes with Hunter. A lopsided smirk stretches across his handsome face. My knees start to tremble, and goosebumps ghost over my skin. The way he's looking at me sends shivers up and down my spine.

When they turn to leave, I follow them through the crowd. I swear my curiosity is going to get me killed or in very deep shit one of these days. Like my mom always says, I'm too nosy for my own good. Right before the end of the dock, Wolf and the other guys veer off to the side and meet the other outside another building, but they're not alone. I watch as the newcomer struggles and realize that one of the Four Horsemen has a hand wrapped around his arm. Hunter quickly pulls a gun from the back waistband of his jeans and aims it at the man. The one who interrupted my conversation with Wolf earlier steps up and grabs the man's other arm so that he's unable to flee. That's when three of them escort the man into the building while Hunter keeps the gun trained on him. I'm too far away to hear anything that's being said, but I can hear my heart beating in my ears. Whatever I just saw can't be good. As if he can hear my thoughts, Hunter turns and locks eyes with me.

I'm frozen; crouched down beside an industrial garbage can. Heart racing as I wonder if he'll aim the gun at me next. But he just slips it back inside his waistband

and turns, disappearing inside the building. The rational part of my brain is screaming at me to run in the other direction, to get back to the party and find Julie. But my curiosity is eating away at me again. The scene I just saw should scare me. What the hell is Hunter doing with a gun and what are they planning on doing to that poor man?

Just as I'm about to step out of my not-so-hidden hiding spot, my phone pings with a message.

Julie: Where'd you disappear to? We're moving the party to Connor's. You in?

I'm assuming Connor is the guy she was talking to when I decided to go exploring on my own. I chew on my bottom lip and weigh my options. I could sneak in there and hope none of them notice me, but seeing as how Hunter already saw me out here that doesn't seem like the greatest idea. Or I can just ask Julie what her stepbrother and his friends are up to. Owning a gun in Canada isn't illegal. It is, however, illegal to conceal and carry. There is another option. Since Hunter already saw me, I can just come right out and ask him. I snort. And pigs really do fly.

I text Julie back.

Me: Yeah. Be right there.

CHAPTER FIVE

HUNTER

I'M FINDING IT hard to conceal my grin as the four of us stand in front of our newest prey. I don't know whether to find it cute or pathetic that she thought she could hide against the dumpster and we wouldn't know she was there. All of us have been trained to be hyper aware of our surroundings from a young age. It comes with being part of our families. It was hard not to give away that we knew she was there while we were dealing with a pest, but as soon as the others had entered the building, I made sure that she knew that we knew she was there. I didn't have to be close to her to hear her sharp intake of breath when my eyes collided with hers. I saw it. Wished I could feel it under my fingers as I pushed inside her.

Jagger subtly bumps my shoulder with his. I mentally give my head a shake and force it back into the game. We always have to be on point. If we relax just a little, it could mean the difference between life or death for us. As one, like we've done hundreds of times before, we pull down the black masks over our faces. Wolf starts us off like he always does.

"Beware."

"Beware."

"Beware."

"Beware," we all chant.

"What the fuck kind of sick joke is this?" Our prey yells, eyes jumping between the four of us. We ignore him as we continue.

"Beware of the dark, for that's where the monsters lurk."

"Want to play a game?" Jagger says from my right. His voice cold and dead with just a hint of crazy.

"We'll even give you a head start," Wolf taunts.

I take my cue and step up behind our prey to whisper in his ear. "Run."

Like every prey before him, he takes off at a dead run straight to the hiking path into the woods surrounding us.

Kane sighs, "When will they learn to not go for the obvious path?"

"C'mon," Jagger says, glancing at his watch. We usually give them a two-minute head start. "The faster we end this prick, the faster we can be done with this shit."

Together we race towards the woods, breaking off once we enter and each taking a different corner. It doesn't take us long to locate him, and once it's done, I send a single text.

1: It's done.

There's no reply. There never is.

JAGGER

When we get back to the house, we all head to own corners to shower, change and then reconvene in the kitchen where it's Kane's turn to make dinner. It's after midnight but neither of us have eaten much today.

"What are we going to do about the girl?" Wolf asks, stabbing a piece of steak onto his fork.

I throw a glance in Hunter's direction. I could see he was intrigued by her earlier today at the party at the warehouse. He'll never admit it, though. The thing is, he isn't the only one either. I've known these guys my whole life and I can undoubtedly say that we're all feeling this weird pull toward her. It's not entirely welcome either. Our lives have always been laid out for us. What schools we'll attend, friends we associate with, jobs we acquire after graduation. Even our wives have been chosen for us. None of us have a say in any of it. And if we think the Elders will allow us to change the script because of this girl, we're delusional. But I'd be lying if I said there wasn't a thrill attached with having a little fun before we have to settle down and fall in line. There was never any question of if we will do what's expected of us. If the Elders ordained it then it's law in our families. In all the families.

"Nothing," Hunter grunts, gathering more salad on his fork. His steak long gone. "She lives. For now."

We all nod in agreement.

"Think she's going to talk about what she saw?" This from Kane.

"Nah, I don't think so. For all she knows, we had a meeting with a friend." I say with a shrug, leaning against the back of my seat. "but we should keep her close just in case."

Hunter looks over at Kane who's still shoving food into his hole. "Have Julie invite her to the party here tomorrow. It's time to see how brave the little lamb is."

Grins are shared around the table. Depending on how she reacts to us at the party, things will either be changing for the better or for the worst.

CHAPTER SIX

ARLO

LESS THAN TWENTY-FOUR hours.

That's how long I was able to ignore my curiosity of what I saw at the docks and my obsession with the Four Horsemen. There's a reason why I wasn't allowed to watch mystery shows when I was younger. I become obsessed and have to know the outcome before I'm able to move on and do anything else. My addiction to solve puzzles only got worse as I got older and Mom couldn't limit the amount I was exposed to. So, it shouldn't come as a surprise that with the nickname, Four Horsemen, I find them intriguing.

I flip onto my front on my beach towel and pull my hair over one shoulder. Since it's still ridiculously hot in the GTA, Julie and I decided to hit up Coburg beach for a few hours today to get some sun. I also may have an ulterior motive for wanting to see her.

"Why the Four Horsemen?" I ask, picking at my nails, worried about her reaction.

She shifts on her towel beside me and readjusts her sunglasses on her pert nose. "I don't know. They've been inseparable ever since they were born. The way Mom tells it, they were too destructive to be called the four musketeers. You could tell where they had been by how bad a room was in disarray."

She pauses before opening her mouth to speak again but closes it. I get the feeling there might be more to it than that, though.

"But you and Kane are stepsiblings?"

"Yeah," she says, tilting her face back further to get more of the sun's rays. "I've never met my bio dad, and Rod and Kane have always been around."

I flip around onto my back and wiggle around a bit trying to get comfortable again. We're quiet for a while just soaking up the sun and the sound of the waves and people around us. Julie's phone pings and she flips over so she can reach into her beach bag to retrieve it. My curiosity is eating away at me, wondering if it's one of the Four Horsemen who texted her. I really do have a problem. But thankfully I don't have to wait long.

She sighs, typing something on her phone and then shoves it back into her bag. "My brother's throwing a party tonight. You down?"

"Sure" I shrug like it's no big deal, but internally I'm squealing like a five-year-old. I shouldn't be as curious about these four guys as I am. What I need to do is focus all my energy on school and not flunking out my first year of university, but there's something about them that I just can't let go.

Julie and I stay at the beach for a couple more hours before we decide to hit up a fast-food drive-thru before heading back to her place. I use her shower to wash away the lake water and sand. Unfortunately, my clothes are full of sand and there's no way that she'll want to drive me home so I can change before heading to the party. Plus, the idea of putting on dirty clothes after I've just had a shower is gross. I end up borrowing a black skirt and tank top from her since those are the only articles of clothing she owns that happen to fit me. She's shorter and skinnier than me so the knee length skirt on her is more like a mini skirt on me, barely dropping below my ass cheeks. The top is a little tight, but not too bad. Since we wear the same shoe size, she lets me borrow a pair red heels so that I don't have to wear the worn flip flops I had on earlier. Truthfully, I would've preferred the flip flops but I can't deny that the heels are cute. I just hope I don't break an ankle or my neck in them.

The house the party is being held at isn't too far from the university campus and Julie's apartment, neither of us wants to walk there in this humidity so we decide to take the TTC. The train isn't too crowded by the time we get on so we're able to find two seats together. As soon as we sit down, Julie immediately pulls up the latest book she's reading on her phone. Since she's distracted, I decide to do some social media stalking.

By the time our stop comes, my efforts have been for naught. The only one who has some semblance of a social media presence is Kane and it's very limited to a few pictures on Instagram. How the hell do a group of men in their early twenties not have any sort of online presence?!

The station we hop off at is packed with students and others hitting the town on a Friday night so Julie grabs hold of my hand and tugs me along behind her. We race up the stairs to the street level and then she takes a right. The street is a little less crowded so I'm able to drop her hand and walk beside her. We walk for a couple blocks. The duplexes with triangle roof arches on either side of the street turn into smaller, more modern looking homes. The further down we go, the squarer and more uniformed-looking the homes become. It's a little sad to see how the curb appeal of homes has changed over the years, and not for the better. Especially in a culture diverse city like Toronto. The homes used to be beautiful with character and now they look like the same cookie-cutter, toaster-looking, design.

Eventually, Julie turns right again and leads us up the front walk of one of those cookie-cutter houses. This one bigger than the rest. The outside of the house looks like it's made from giant slabs of cement with cut outs for the windows and door, which is painted a black matte. There are already other university students spilling out onto the front lawn and standing around the door so we make our way inside without knocking, and immediately make our way through an open layout living and dining room, passing a spiral staircase to the kitchen. The music isn't as loud on this side of the house as it is in the front which makes it easier to hear Julie when she leans over and asks me if I want a drink. I nod and follow her over to the stone countertop where various drinks from beer to wine to whiskey are laid out as well as chasers. Julie goes for the whiskey and pours a double shot into two red plastic cups before topping it with Dr. Pepper. Just like last night, once she makes sure I have a drink in my hand she moves off to chat with a group of people I've never met before.

I take the opportunity to explore the house a little. Despite the cold look of the exterior, the inside looks like it would be cozy if there weren't about a hundred students crammed inside and outside. There's a group gathered around a billiards table in the living room. It isn't hard for me to picture Kane shooting pool with the other guys in the evenings or on weekends. I make my way to the back of the house again and push open the sliding glass door, closing it behind me again. After being in the loud house, it's nice and quiet out here. The sun's beginning to set and there's a slight breeze in the air now. I kick off the heels Julie made me wear and make sure to line them up somewhere out of the way where they won't get trampled if anyone else decided to venture out this way. With my drink in hand, I walk toward the end of the pool and gingerly lower myself down so as not to spill the liquid. The water is cold when I dip my toes in but soon it warms up and I'm able to lower my legs in further until the water comes up to my calves. For the first time all day, I feel like I can draw in a deep breath and relax. Despite being in the middle of one of the biggest and busiest cities in Canada, I feel like time slows down here… maybe even stills.

That is until rustling sounds from somewhere behind me. I turn to glance over my shoulder but can't see anything beyond the shadows of the trees lining the fence. When I don't hear anything else, I figure it's just a squirrel or a bird or something and turn back to the pool. The water glows purple from the coloured underwater lights. I slowly swirl my legs in circles in the water but stop when I hear a moan followed by whispered curses and then,

"Christ, Wolf. Just like that."

My cheeks heat. That most definitely was not a female voice. Feeling like I'm creeping on their privacy by staying out here. I try to silently remove my feet from the water and stand up. I'm about half way back to the sliding glass door when another very masculine voice groans out, "Jagger."

CHAPTER SEVEN

WOLF

THE PARTY IS a rager, but then again it always is on a Friday night. It's no secret that our place is the place to be for Queen's University students on a Friday. We pay the local OPP, Ontario Provincial Police, handsomely to look the other way, since there's no doubt going to be a few freshman that will undoubtedly show up and be drinking and I refuse to go to jail for some underage drinking idiots. I'm reclined back on one side of the leather couch, one arm strewn across the back while the other rests on the arm. Beer in one hand and a beautiful chick kneeling between my spread thighs. Her blonde hair looks like a halo around her head with the way the light from the standing lamp glows behind her. And maybe that's why I can't seem to get into it, no matter how hard she sucks. I'm just not feeling it. Fucking halo. It's all a bunch of mythological bullshit. Angels don't wear halos. Not unless it's a halo of self-righteousness. The wings are the only thing they got right.

Jagger bumps my shoulder so I turn to him, completely ignoring what's going on between my legs. *Give it up, Sweetheart.*

"Yo, man. You alright?"

I give him a clipped nod and take a drag of my beer, and wince. It's warm as shit. "I'm gonna go get another. You want one?" I ask him, pushing the blonde off me and zipping up my jeans. Jagger raises a questioning brow but just lifts his empty bottle up in thanks. I head towards the back of the house, pushing people out of my way as I go and ignoring the curses thrown my way. While I get how important these Friday night parties are to help solidify our place at the university, I don't see why we couldn't have taken one fucking night off. Especially after what happened earlier tonight.

When I make it over to the fridge, I pull it open and start reaching for a cold beer but stop, closing the door and reaching for something harder instead. I slam back a shot of vodka straight from the bottle and then another before pouring a shot into a red cup. I was off my game tonight. I'm never fucking off my game, but there was something about what we did that's not sitting right with me. Bracing my hands on the edge of the counter I let my head fall forward and try to ignore the sounds of the party going on around me.

Goddammit!

If Jagger hadn't been right at my back this evening, the whole thing would've gone to shit and it would've all been because I hesitated for a split-fucking-second.

A hand lands on my shoulder and grips it, but I shrug it off already knowing who it is. I pull open the fridge again and pull out a cold beer, and hand it to him. Jagger takes it from me but his stare doesn't waiver from my face.

"Let's go outside," he says.

I fold my arms across my chest but don't make a move toward the sliding glass door behind me. "I'm fine, man. Let it go." I pick up the red cup I had poured the extra shot of vodka into, but Jagger snatches my wrist before I can bring the cup to my lips.

He steps up closer to me until I can feel his breath on my lips. His eyes blazing a weird mix of green and gold. "Outside. Now."

I shiver but uncross my arms and turn to lead the way outside. Jagger brushes passed me and doesn't stop until he's disappearing through the trees that line the property, just before the neighbour's fence. I don't know why the fuck for. It's our place, who gives a fuck what we do, but like a good little boy I follow him. As soon as I clear the trees, he's gripping me by the front of my shirt and hauling me back against the trunk of a tree. My back hits the bark with an *oomph.* I might be a couple inches taller, and weigh about twenty pounds heavier, but Jagger possesses a strength you wouldn't suspect by just looking at him. He wedges a knee between my thighs and presses up tight against my quickly hardening dick. The hand that was wrapped in my shirt moves to curl around my throat while his other hand grips the short strands of hair at the back of my head and yanks on them. Pain explodes, but it's a welcome distraction from the mess my head was in back in the house.

"You need to let that shit go," he snarls in my face, but there's heat behind his eyes. I feel him growing hard against my thigh. Of course, he knew where my thoughts were at. He always does.

"You and me both know that something wasn't right about this one. Hell, Hunter and Kane know it too."

Jagger searches my eyes for what feels like eternity and then loosens his hold on my hair and drops his forehead to mine. He releases a long breath while lifting his hand from around my throat and moving it to my hip, tugging me closer into him.

"We know, but you also know that we have to keep playing this game their way for now. Until…" he trails off, but I finish his thought for him.

"Until we know if it's her."

He nods. I dig the pads of my fingers tighter into his hips and pull him even closer which causes his knee to press tighter into my groin. I groan and Jagger curses. The four of us have been on this earth long enough to know that sexuality isn't a one size fits all. That it's fluid. We've often hooked up with each other and/or brought others into our beds. However, recently, we've all agreed that it doesn't feel right anymore to share our beds with anyone else. But we couldn't understand why. And then we saw her, and everything began slowly clicking into place.

I work Jagger's belt open and unzip his jeans before falling to my knees in the cold dirt. He groans, bracing a palm against the tree while his other hand guides my head to his dick. He's not wearing any underwear so I don't waste any time wrapping my lips around his thick shaft and twirling my tongue around the head.

"Christ, Wolf. Just like that."

I grip the base of his cock in my fist and double my efforts to get him off. It doesn't take long before he's shooting down my throat and I swallow every last drop before cleaning him off with my tongue. Jagger pulls me up by my hair and slams his mouth down on mine. His hand goes back to my cock, slipping under my boxers this time. I wrap an arm around his neck and deepen the kiss while he jacks me off like his life depends on it. I'm about to come in my pants like a horny teenager, but I don't give a fuck. I groan low in my throat and he eats it up, tightening his fist and jacking me faster. Holy fucking shit.

"Jagger." His name is like a plea on my lips and seconds later I'm spilling all over his hand and in my shorts.

"I think we had an audience," he chuckles when we've somewhat caught our breath.

I'm too busy watching him lick my cum from his fingers, that I almost miss what he's saying. "Who?" I ask, looking back towards the house, but then I see her… just her back as she scurries through the open glass door.

Jagger and I pull ourselves together and then head back inside to go in search of the other half of our quad. It doesn't come as a surprise to us when we find Hunter and Kane in the same position we were in not too long ago. Jagger grabs us all some beers while Hunter and Kane get cleaned up and then they meet me in the library just off the main living room. During renovations, we made sure that this room as well as our bedrooms were insulted and sound proofed to the max to prevent nosy fuckers from eavesdropping. This conversation should've waited until tomorrow when the house wasn't filled with university students, but from just one look at my best friends it's obvious to me that none of us will be getting any sleep tonight if we can't work through what happened now.

You see, the students and faculty at Queen's like to joke around and call us the Four Horsemen. It was a stupid nickname that Kane's human step mother christened us with when we were 'kids.' Everywhere the four of us went, we left destruction in our wake. No one but the four of us and The Elders know just how real the nickname really is. In fact, it's not a nickname at all.

The library is something you would expect to see in a library at a Gentlemen's Club. Tall, hand crafted mahogany wood bookcases take up three of the four walls. Each filled with books about our history and bible editions dating back centuries, as well as a few other books thrown in. Kane is the avid romance reader out of the three of us. A stone fireplace takes up the entire last wall. Four leather wingback chairs sit in a semi-circle facing the monstrosity. I personally didn't see the point in having a fireplace this big but it was the one thing Hunter wanted. I guess it reminded him of home or some shit.

We all take our seats around the fireplace but no one moves or speaks for several long minutes. Eventually, Hunter leans over to grab a remote on the coffee table and turns up the music out in the main house for extra precaution. The books on the shelves jump with the thump of the base. Being who we are, our hearing is impeccable. Even without the sound proofing in this room, we'd be able to hear each other fine without yelling or leaning in close.

"Do we know anything about him?" Hunter asks.

Neither of us have to ask who *him* is. The man we were told to hunt this evening.

Jagger pushes up from his chair and saunters over to the bar on the left of the fireplace. "Bryan Carlson. Forty-two. Divorced. Father of two," he rattles off the information like it's nothing. Only the three of us know that it's not nothing. It's eating him alive just like it is the rest of us. "His history is clean. Not so much as a black mark." He makes his way back to us with a glass of bourbon in his hand. His beer from earlier long forgotten.

Kane curses, his fingers beginning to curl in a fist on his thigh before he stops himself and relaxes them. I blow out a relieved breath. None of us wants an accidental war to break out in the main house.

"Why the fuck were we sent after him then? Unless, The Elders are suddenly using us to kill innocents now," I growl, tightening my own fist. At least if I'm to do it there's no possibility of a war starting.

Hunter rakes a hand through his hair as we all look to him. He looks just as beat as the rest of us, but he'll never admit it.

"I don't know, but this ends now. I'm done being their puppets."

We all nod in agreement. It's not the first time those fuckers have tried to use us for their personal enjoyment. The last time it happened, we almost lost Kane. That is not something either of us wishes to relive.

Jagger sighs beside me, leaning back in his seat and crossing an ankle over his knee. "We all know that's not going to happen. As much as I can't wait to be out from under their thumb, we do have to continue playing by their rules if we ever want to be truly free."

Kane huffs, crossing his arms and glaring at Jagger, even though we all know he's right. "We don't even know if the letter is right, and even if it is, how do we know that it's her that'll bring it true? I refuse to play personal hitman for a bunch of ancients."

"The letter could be another sick joke they're playing on us," I say, draining the rest of my beer and getting up to pour something stronger. "For all we know, he was one of them." He as in the one who wrote the letter addressed to the four of us.

All eyes swing to Hunter then, but his face is cold, stoic, giving nothing away to the fact that his 'dad' is pulling all of our strings and neither one of us knows what the reason behind the latest game. We decided long ago to start referring to the hunts as games. It makes it seem less… murdery.

"Regardless," Jagger interjects, taking some of the attention off Hunter. "We need to be more diligent in vetting the names now that we know they aren't all guilty of something."

We all agree and then one by one head back out to the main house and upstairs to bed. Neither of us giving a fuck that the house is still filled with students. They could burn down the house and the four of us would shrug and go, "see y'all next Friday." That's the thing with living as long as we have, nothing fazes you anymore.

CHAPTER EIGHT

ARLO

BACK AT MY apartment a few blocks away, I still can't get the sounds of what I heard out of my head. It was… unexpected. And hot. Unexpectedly hot. Of course, I didn't stick around long enough for Wolf and Jagger to catch me listening to them having sex, but as I turn the shower on and wait for it to heat, I briefly wonder what it would've been like if they had caught me. Would they threaten me? Were they even out? Oh god, what if they caught me and found out that I *liked* it. Would they make fun of me? Or what if… I pump a couple drops of my shower gel onto a loofa and begin running it over my body. What if the thought of someone overhearing them turned them on as much as it turned me on to hear them?

I run a soapy palm over my belly, shivering at the touch, and then slide it lower as I wonder what it would be like if they invited me to join them. I suck in a quick breath as my fingers find the little nub between my thighs. I moan, cupping a breast and lean against the cold tile of the shower.

"You like that, baby?" Jagger purrs, taking over the gentle massage of my breasts.

"She's so fucking wet," Wolf says from between my thighs and then licks up my slit.

"Perfect," Hunter growls from my right, sliding a hand between my legs to assist Wolf.

Kane hums on my left, dipping his head down to lick around my other nipple.

"Oh god," I groan, fighting to stay above the waves of pleasure threatening to drown me. The sensations attacking my body are too much. So many hands, so many mouths and tongues. I have no idea which way is up anymore. "Please." My voice is a breathy plea. A plea for what? I don't know. To stop? For more and to never stop?

Hunter chuckles, moving behind me and forcing me to bend over until I'm hunched over Wolf's head. Jagger and Kane continue their ministrations. Toying with my nipples and running their hands all over my body as Hunter slides a finger over my hole. My whole body freezes. I've never done that, but right now I wouldn't say no to him. I want to do that. When he runs the pad of his finger over it again, I moan and push back into him. Silently begging for more. The next time it isn't his finger that rubs my hole, but the head of his cock. I feel Wolf's warm breath there too and then Hunter groans deep, his fingers digging deeper into the skin at my hips. The image of Wolf sucking Hunter off to get him ready to breach me is so fucking hot. I'm not sure if I'll last much longer. Then Hunter's cock is back and pushing passed the tight ring of muscle while Wolf eats my pussy like it's quite possibly his last meal on earth.

A strong, masculine arm wraps around my middle and pulls me up so my back is plastered against Hunter's chest. He swiftly moves my hair off my shoulder and tugs my head back, exposing my throat to his roaming mouth.

"You going to come for us, Little Lamb?" He rasps into my ear.

I bite down on my bottom lip and nod furiously while rocking my hips back and forth. With every forward motion, I get Wolf's tongue deeper and with every backward motion, Hunter's cock slides deeper into my ass. Jagger and Kane grin as they continue to nip and suck my nipples.

"Oh god, oh god, oh god," I ramble as my orgasm rushes up and drags me under. I'm unable to fight the pull anymore and let wave after intense wave wash over me. Hunter pulls out and then I feel warm cum land across the top of my ass. Jagger and Kane both come across my stomach and I look down to see that Wolf has also come on the shower floor.

I slump back against the tile, completely deflated and half disappointed that it was all in my imagination and half grateful that that's all it was. I don't know if I could ever handle that type of intensity in real life.

I finish my shower and rinse off before stepping out and grabbing a towel. Once I'm dry and dressed in loose PJ pants and an old band t-shirt, I crawl into the middle of my queen bed and promptly fall asleep.

The next morning comes way too fucking fast. Blurry eyed, I drag myself out of bed and pull on a pair of skinny jeans and an old Harry Potter shirt. The neckline is so stretched from years of wear that it slides down my shoulder. I don't bother trying to pull it up again, it'll be useless anyway. I grab my laptop bag and the textbooks I'll need and absently wave a goodbye to my roommate before leaving the condo. I half stumble down the half block to the coffee shop, ignoring the amused looks I know I'm getting along the way. Coffee. Need coffee.

Brynn, the barista gives me a knowing look when it's my turn to step up to the counter. "The usual?" she asks, with a grin.

I nod, pulling out my wallet. "Please," I say, then pause. "Actually, make it a venti this time."

"Late night?" she asks, entering my order into the computer and then scanning my card.

You have no idea. Images of what Wolf and Jagger were doing behind that tree last night begin playing through my mind followed by what I did in the shower and the realness of how it felt. I shiver, and then shrug at Brynn's question. "Something like that," I say, moving over to the pickup counter and looking around.

The coffee shop isn't as busy as it usually is at this time on a Saturday morning, but the weather is still nice out so I can't really blame anyone for wanting to be outside and enjoying the sunshine before the cold starts to move in. GTA winters can be brutal. Last winter, Oshawa had several days of non-stop freezing rain which made getting anywhere a challenge. Our entire front porch was one big slip and slide. I even had to go down the three steps on my butt or risk falling and breaking something. Ice and I do not get along. Like, at all. Mom tried for years to get me into ice skating when I was a kid. I'm pretty coordinated, but when I was on the ice it was like I was a baby duck who hadn't learnt how to use its feet yet. She found it amusing. I, on the other hand, did not. Especially because the last time we went to the rink, I fell on my ass and slid across the rink and right into my crush at the time, sending him into the boards. It was horrifying. Even years later in grade 12, every time I would see him in the hallway, I would duck and run away. I'm convinced he thought I was some kind of weirdo but the humiliation was strong after the rink incident. I vowed to myself never again would I be caught dead in a pair of ice skates.

When my order is called, I grab the drink and head over to my favourite table in the far corner. This spot is kind of hidden from the rest of the shop but is right next to one of the windows so I can people watch when I need to give my brain a break from studying. I found this place shortly after I moved in and it's been a godsend whenever I need to get out of the condo or just need some me time. My roommate is great and all, and technically I don't really need one but the company is great. It's just sometimes I like my alone time.

I pull up my notes from the biology lab the other day after opening my laptop and the ecology textbook and get to work studying for the midterm coming up in two weeks.

I've just started drawing out the process of mitosis when someone sits on the bench beside me and rests their arms on the small round table. I pause what I was doing and look up at the newcomer from under a section of brown hair that came loose from my messy bun I threw it in this morning.

He either doesn't notice me staring at him or he doesn't care because Kane continues to lean in close to my laptop and read what's on the screen while every so often, glancing down at the open text book and the notes I was taking. This is the closest I've been to any of them and my belly does an excited flip. He's wearing black athletic pants and a light grey workout tank. His muscled arms are on full display, and the way they flex every time he leans just a tad closer to the screen makes my mouth water. I never understood why women found veins sexy, but now I know. God, what I wouldn't give to run my tongue along those long lines.

"It's rude to stare."

I snap my jaw closed, not realizing until then that my mouth was hanging open while I ogled him, and swallow hard. My throat suddenly feeling really dry. "I, um, I'm sorry?" I ask, still trying to clear the fog from my brain.

Kane grins. His golden whiskey coloured eyes lighting up in amusement as his attention moves from the biology notes to me. His blond hair is spiked in the front but I suspect that's more from him running a hand through his hair than the way it was styled.

"It's rude to stare," he says again, but doesn't make a move to look away either.

And now we're in a staring contest in the middle of the coffee shop. Well, not the *middle* middle but… you get the idea. I huff, breaking the stare down first and making him chuckle. My cheeks heat and not out of embarrassment but because I could easily stare into those golden eyes for hours.

"It's also rude to just invite yourself to sit down," I snap back.

"Maybe," he shrugs, fingering the corner of my textbook. "Or maybe I'm just trying to save you from failing the mitosis lab."

"What are you talking about?"

He points to the diagram I had been drawing before he sat down. "That's the process of meiosis."

I glance down, my brows pulling down in a frown as I take in the diagram I drew and then the identical one in the textbook.. "No, it's not."

He laughs. "Yes, it is," he argues then turns the page of the textbook back to the previous one. He flips it back and forth a couple times before picking at the edge of the page. My jaw drops again when the single page splits into two. "They were stuck together," he announces, like I hadn't been watching him pry them apart seconds ago.

I drop my hands in my lap and groan. "I'm such an idiot. So much for trying to study ahead."

Kane slams the textbook close and then closes the lid of my laptop. "C'mon. Let's go."

"Uh, go where? I need to study."

He stands up, throwing his coffee cup in the garbage close by and then turns a raised eyebrow at me. "You have mid-terms already?"

I blush and reel back a bit. "Not exactly."

He stacks the textbook and notepad on top of the closed laptop and gathers them in his arms. "If you want these back, you'll come with me," he says mimicking Arnold in Terminator.

"That was terrible." Since he's left me no choice, I gather my backpack from beside me and scoot out from the corner. He hands me back my stuff and watches while I put them in my backpack and zip it up.

"What are you talking about? That was *the* best Terminator impression." He takes my hand in his and pulls me out of the coffee shop and over to a metallic Jeep Wrangler.

I roll my eyes. “Keep telling yourself that. Where are we going?”

“It’s a surprise.” He grins, opening the passenger side door for me and playfully bowing as I pull myself up into the jeep. At 5’6”, I’m not short by any means, but the jeep is lifted so even I have to use the running board, in order to get in.

Kane jumps into the driver’s side, throws the SUV in drive and peels out of the parking lot like the Ontario Provincial Police is on his ass. We’ve just merged onto highway 400 when he glances down at the laptop bag I stowed by my feet when we left the coffee shop.

“You don’t by any chance have a swim suit in there, do ya?”

I snort out a laugh and barely restrain myself from rolling my eyes. “Not unless it magically turned into a Mary Poppin’s bag.”

Kane's shoulders visibly deflate and his lips turn down in a pout.

"Oh my god!" I snicker. "You really hoped it had."

He mock gasps, pressing a hand on his chest and making a giggle burst from me. "I have no idea what you're talking about."

"You're a closeted Disney nerd." I can't help the wide grin that splits my face.

"Am not!" He says sounding offended. "There's nothing closeted about me."

I throw my head back against the seat and howl with laughter. Tears are streaming down my face and my sides hurt from how hard I'm laughing.

"What's so funny?" Kane asks, checking his right blind spot and switching lanes.

"Just never pictured you as a Disney fan that's all," I reply once I've got my laughter under control.

"Yeah, well," he starts as he takes an exit ramp and the light mood disappears. "There's a lot about us you don't know."

I watch him with a new found curiosity as he navigates the SUV into a mall parking lot, not really sure how to take his last statement. Considering this is only the second time I've interacted with any one of the four, he's right I don't know them. But I have a feeling that there is a lot more meaning behind those words. Kane parks the vehicle and jumps out. I follow closely behind him after scrambling down from the passenger side.

"What are we doing here?" I ask, once we've crossed the parking lot and he holds the door to the mall open for me.

"Getting you a swim suit. Why else would be here?" He says, and there's so much about that statement that I have questions about, but before I can ask any of them, he adds, "you can't very well go wake boarding in jeans and flip flops, now can you?"

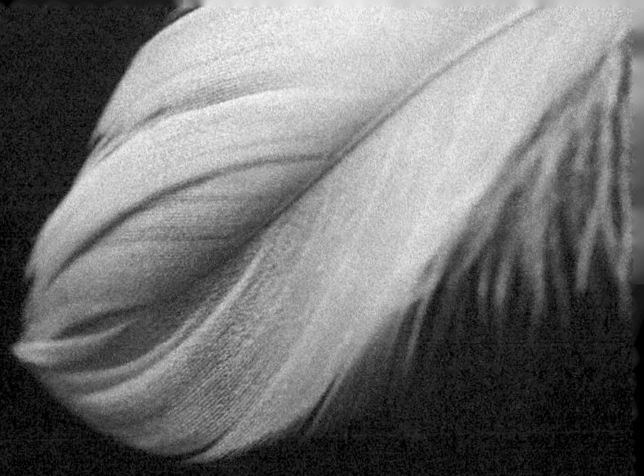

CHAPTER NINE

ARLO

HIS WORDS AND the casualty with which he says them catches me off guard and I pause, rooted to the spot in the middle of the walkway. Shoppers curse as they're forced to walk around me but I can't get my feet to continue walking. Several seconds pass before Kane realizes that I'm no longer walking beside him. He stops and turns around to come back to where I'm still standing.

"What? What's wrong?" Kane takes hold of my upper arms, his eyes roaming over every inch of my body. He's so close that I can smell whatever aftershave or cologne he used this morning.

I know the action isn't sexual but it still sends a shiver down my spine. Just the fact that he seems so worried that something could've happened to me in the few seconds when I wasn't beside him. His concerned eyes lift to meet mine and for a split second I forget that we're standing in the middle of a very busy mall.

"Why are we going wake boarding?" I blurt, welcoming the crash back down to reality. Disappointment settles heavy in my gut when he removes his hands from my arms and takes a step back.

Kane ignores my question and turns back around. "C'mon, this place is a mad house and we still have an hour to get to Wasaga Beach."

Giving up on ever getting answers from him, I go about following him around the mall. When the first store he stops in front of has a display rack of barely there biki-ni's — if you can even call them that — I snort, roll my eyes and continue moving on to the next store making him try to catch up with me.

"What was wrong with that store?" Kane asks when we stop outside of a different one a few storefronts down.

"I have boobs," I say, wandering over to the swim suit section in the back.

"Yeah, so?"

I flip through the limited selection of tops for my bra size and pick out a plain black one and a royal blue one of the same design. "Those ones wouldn't cover anything."

Kane stares at me with his head cocked to the side like he's having trouble figuring out what the problem is. The genuine confused look on his face would be cute if it wasn't so typical man. When he still hasn't clued in as to why this is a problem, I decide to put him out of his misery.

"I'm not about to have my top come off if or when I bail on the water."

A slow, sexy smirk pulls at the corners of his lips. "I wouldn't mind."

"Of course, you wouldn't," I sigh, crouching down to pick out some bottoms.

I find a pair of high waisted ones and short shorts both in black and add them to the pile. When I browse the rest of the store and doesn't turn up anything else of interest, I head on back toward the changing rooms. Kane right behind me. Before I can close the door, he's pushing his way in.

"Um, no," I say, stopping him with a hand on his chest.

"What? Why?" Kane looks downright crest fallen that I won't let him watch me get changed.

"First, because I don't know you and second, I don't feel like getting arrested today. Thank you very much."

He snorts, leaning a shoulder against the door jam and folding his arm over his chest. And why are my eyes so drawn to the size of his arms?

"We won't get arrested." He studies me for what feels like an hour and then gives a sharp nod as he straightens up from the door. "But fine. I'll wait out here."

I close and lock the door behind him and then go through the motions of trying the swim wear on over my underwear. I'm surprised when both fit perfectly. Usually, it takes me forever and a lot of tears before I'm satisfied with a swim suit. But a quick glance at the price tags lets me know that I can only buy one set. When I'm fully dressed again, I head out of the changing rooms, not seeing Kane sitting on the love seat that's provided. I spot him over at the sunglass carousel when I make my way up to the cash register and let the associate know that I'll just be taking the black top and high-waisted bottoms.

"We'll take them all," Kane interjects, adding a couple pairs of sunglasses, flip flops, men's swim shorts, and a couple pairs of water shoes to the mix as well.

I blanche. There must be almost a thousand dollars' worth of stuff here. "Kane, I can pay for my own stuff."

He leans an elbow on the glass display case by the cash register and looks over his shoulder at me. "You can. But you're not going to." I move to argue with him, but his next words stop me. "You can pay for dinner if you want."

I narrow my eyes at him and his full lips curve up in a crooked smile. Fucking hell. I relent and let him pay for my swim suit. When the associate tells him the total, her eyes go wide when he hands her a black credit card. Not going to lie, mine do too. What the hell is a university student doing with a black credit card? *Maybe mommy and daddy are stinking rich.*

The sales associate bags up our order and beams up at Kane when she goes to hand him the bag. He winks at her and the urge to throat punch her comes out of nowhere, taking me by surprise. Then, with the bag in one hand Kane grabs my hand with his free one and pulls me out of the store. We practically speed walk back through the mall and across the parking lot to where he parked his Jeep. He holds the passenger door open for me again and then hands me the shopping bag before shutting the door and jogging around the vehicle. He curses when he starts the engine and gets a look at the time display on the deck.

"If you're not okay with speed then you might want to close your eyes," he says, once we hit the on ramp for highway 400 again.

"Wha-" Before the word had fully left my mouth, Kane begins weaving through traffic, barely leaving an inch of space between cars as he switches back and forth between lanes. I shut my eyes but then quickly open them again when the nausea becomes too much. But I wish I hadn't because as soon as I open them, I see the tail lights of the car in front of us light up. Kane slams on the breaks, harrowingly missing rear ending the vehicle. "Shit. Shit. Shit."

The cocky fucker grins over at me. "We were fine. I had it under control."

Words are failing me right now. I want to wail at him that just because he thinks he had everything under control doesn't mean that it was true. He can't, after all, control the drivers around us. Case in point, the driver in front of us who slammed on his brakes which caused Kane to slam on his. Thank God there wasn't any one following too closely behind us. My heart is threatening to beat out of my chest with all the adrenaline coursing through my body. Too close.

Once traffic starts moving again, Kane thankfully dials down the crazy and stops zig zagging through traffic. That is until we get stuck behind a driver going ten under the speed limit and he switches lanes to pass the guy. We make it to Wasaga Beach around noon and about twenty minutes earlier than we should've. Kane pulls into the parking lot of Wasaga Marine and cuts the engine.

"I'll keep watch while you get changed," he says and then slips out of the driver's side, closing the door behind me and leaning his back against it.

Even at 6'2, the Jeep is too lifted for his stature to fully block the window but that also means that it's harder for anyone to look in. After pulling two of the four pieces from the bag, I lean back in the passenger seat and lift my hips to shimmy my jeans and underwear down to my ankles and then use my feet to slide them all the way off. With the bottoms on, I reach around under my shirt and undo the clasp on my bra, pulling the straps through the sleeves and then the bra through the bottom of my shirt. Getting the top of the swim suit on is the tricky part, but after some maneuvering, I'm able to get it on. After getting redressed, I jump out of the Jeep and meet Kane on the other side where his head is bent as he concentrates on his phone.

"My turn."

Thinking that he's going to do the same and jump back into the jeep to change, I don't turn around immediately when he opens the door and starts ruffling through the bag, but then he's pushing down his jeans and I get an eye full of his ass. And god, what an ass it is. I squeak and turn around, covering my eyes for extra precaution even as the bastard laughs behind me.

"You could've warned me first!"

"But where would the fun in that be?" Several more seconds pass before I hear the slam of the door and beeps as the alarm is being set, but I still don't turn around. Somehow, I don't put it past Kane to not be completely covered up. "I'm decent, Princess."

"Thank God for small favours," I mumble, following him down to the marina.

"There is nothing small about me," he teases with that crooked grin on his face.

I get the impression that Kane is the youngest of the four. I sense that he has a deep longing to be accepted by those around him, especially by Hunter, Wolf, and Jagger even though they already do. At least, that's the impression I get from the limited times I've been around them in the last week. But I've overheard enough of their conversations in class to know that they see Kane as one of them.

Kane greets a guy dressed in a Wasaga Marine uniform and they chat for a bit before the guy points to a boat in one of the slips and then slaps Kane on the back before heading back into the store. I follow him down the dock to the boat and he takes my hand, helping me on. The thought of spending the whole day with Kane sends a thrill through me, but as I start to ask him if anyone else will be joining us, I hear voices coming down the dock. Ones I recognize. I guess I have my answer.

CHAPTER TEN

KANE

SPENDING THE LAST hour or so with Charlotte was unexpected to say the least. She could've easily told me to fuck off when I practically demand she come with me. Hell, I think most chicks would. She barely knows me. But she jumped into my Jeep like she hadn't a care in the world. I frown at the metal wheel in front of me. We'd have to talk about that. As soon as The Elders realize that the four of us have taken a vested interest in her – and they will eventually. We won't be able to keep them off her scent for long now – she'll need to be careful about who she trusts. Whistles from down on the dock catches my attention and I grin. Gangs all here. I glance at my watch, and early too. I wince. I *may* have lamented a bit about the part of us being late and me needing to speed through traffic to get here on time. In truth, adrenaline is to me what a cup of coffee in the morning is to most people. I needed to see how she would react to a bit of speed. I wasn't lying, though, when I said that I had it all under control when we very nearly missed rearing ending the douche in the sports car in front of us. Who the fuck slams on their brakes like that on the highway!?

As soon as the guys and Jules are on board, and Wolf has untied us, I maneuver the boat out of the marina and then gun it for the lake. Out of my periphery

I see the girls move towards the front. I open up the boat to see just how fast she can go, and grin when they both squeal and grab hold of the railings. After several minutes, I slow it down again. Not really wanting to get a fine today or have someone accidentally go overboard. Jagger bumps me on the shoulder and then hands me a beer while I try to find a spot for us to set up the board but concentrating is fucking hard when Charlotte pulls up her shirt and deposits it on the bench beside my sister. Her jeans soon following. She does some weird flip with her hair and then secures it in the messiest bun I've ever seen. It should not be as sexy as it is. She looks like a modern-day pin-up girl in the swim suit she picked up today. I chuckle remembering the death glare she gave the sales associate who unashamedly flirted with me. When Jagger asks me what's so funny, I tell him.

"She's not as innocent as she looks, is she?" he says, taking a drink of his beer.

When we're on the boat, we all have a one beer limit just like when we go out to the club. We're not idiots. We know that driving a boat drunk is the same as getting behind the wheel of a vehicle. Plus, neither one of us wants to anger The Elders and the fastest way to do that is to not be available when they call. Getting thrown in jail for a DUI will do that.

I shake my head and slow the boat down when I think I've found the perfect spot far enough away from other boaters. "Nah, don't think she is."

Jagger helps me get everything ready, while Wolf straps in to the life vest first. Charlotte and Jules join us at the back of the boat and take seats on one of the benches.

"Don't get too comfortable, Little Lamb. You're next," Hunter declares before getting in to the water.

The other guys snicker around us and I look over my shoulder expecting to see shock or even horror on her face since watersports aren't for everybody, but instead I find a wide smile and maybe even excitement shining in her eyes.

"Have you been wakeboarding before?" Jagger asks, taking the question right out of my mouth.

Charlotte shrugs, "No, but I surf so it's practically the same thing, right?"

Jules snorts and tries to cover it up with a cough. "Arlo's been swimming with Sharks. She's not afraid of the water like some of the bimbos' you guys have brought on the boat."

That definitely catches our attention. So, our Little Lamb likes to play with the predators, huh? Interesting. I catch a glance at Wolf from the corner of my eye and he grins.

We spend the majority of the day on the lake. Each one of us taking turns either on the board or driving the boat. Charlotte didn't do too bad, although, it took her a couple tries to get up on the board but once she was up, she was amazing. Even doing some tricks and outshining Hunter. Around five, we dock in the marina again and then head to the cabin in separate vehicles. Charlotte and Jules ride with me while Jagger and Wolf ride with Hunter. Charlotte twists around in her seat so that she can chat with Jules on the drive up to the cabin. When the city views begin to give way to forest line streets, her face becomes glued to the window and it's hard to keep the smirk from my face. Fuck, she's adorable.

We all arrive at the cabin in the woods at the same time and Jules shows Charlotte around inside while the guys and I unload the cars with the supplies we had packed earlier this morning before I tracked down Charlotte. Once we have the coolers and grocery bags unpacked in the kitchen, Wolf fires up the grill on the back deck while Hunter gets the steaks ready.

"Ready to get your ass kicked?" I ask Jagger, grabbing one of the controllers from the coffee table and falling onto the seat beside him on the long leather L-shaped couch.

He snorts. "You're on."

He cues up a new NHL 20 game on the PS4 and we play, jostling each other in the arm when the stakes get too close, until the girls come downstairs and Wolf announces that dinner's ready. The conversation around the dinner table is easy, and despite the fact that this is Charlotte's first time hanging with all of us and that I practically kidnapped her today, she's taking it all in stride and doesn't seem too uncomfortable.

"So, how long have you all know each other?" she asks, looking around the table and making eye contact with each of us.

I freeze with my fork half way to my mouth and chance a glance around the table at the other guys who all look like the mirror image of what I'm guessing I look like.

"We all grew up together," Jagger says with a shrug. The lie coming as easy as it has every other time we've said it. Only this time it feels wrong somehow.

I look over at Charlotte and wonder what it would be like to tell someone the truth for once. How would she react? Would she even believe us?

After we've eaten and the dishes are in the dishwasher, Wolf jokingly suggests a game of capture the flag in the dark, in the woods and surprisingly, both girls immediately jump on board. Jules lets Charlotte know that she has an all black outfit she can wear since all Charlotte has are the swimsuits I bought her today and the jeans and t-shirt she was wearing.

I've just changed into black jeans and a black hoodie, and have trudged back down the stairs to the back door when a familiar feeling settles over me and my stomach drops. No. Not now.

I shoot off a text to the rest of the guys — easier than trying to track them down in the cabin — and we all meet in the grassy area in the backyard just before the tree line.

"They have shit timing," Jagger grumbles and we all agree.

Hunter's phone dings with an incoming message outlining the information of our newest prey and the deadline. There's always a fucking deadline.

"What's it say?" I ask, leaning over his shoulder to try and get a look at the encrypted message.

"Sunrise tomorrow." He stuffs the phone back into the pocket of his black sweatpants and runs a hand through his hair. "They're not even giving us twenty-four hours anymore."

"Man, this is bullshit. We're not their fucking errand boys," Wolf seethes, hands on his hips and shoulders heaving with every ragged breath.

"We are until we can lift this god-damn curse."

Jagger laughs, but it's not a funny laugh. More like, he can't believe this shit laugh. "It's been decades and we're no closer to figuring it out now than we were when we first got stuck here."

Just then, a pair of giggles floats over from the back door of the cabin as Jules and Charlotte exit into the cool night air.

As one, we all turn to watch them descend the short flight of stairs.

"She's the key to all this. I don't know how but I'm going to figure it out." He pauses as we all watch the girls' approach and then in a quieter voice so that we're the only ones who hear, he says, "We're done being their puppets."

Murmurs of agreement echo around our small group. As soon as the girls join us, we break off into two teams of three with Charlotte, Wolf and I being on one team and Jules, Jagger, and Hunter on the other. Hunter and Wolf hid the flags earlier before we all met at the marina so after discussing the boundaries of the game the two teams split off and head into the woods. As soon as we break the tree line I stop and turn to Charlotte, tugging up the hood of her black sweater.

"Don't get captured Little Lamb," I say, pulling on the strings to tighten the material around her head. Her long hair is tucked inside the hood and I can barely make out her face in the moonlight shining through the tree tops, but it doesn't take away from how beautiful she is.

Her wide eyes stare up at me as her lips tip up into a grin. "I won't."

"Kane and I will distract Jagger and Hunter so that means you'll just have Jules to get passed. When you get the flag head back to the cabin and we'll meet you there," Wolf instructs her.

Charlotte nods in acknowledgement but then she scrunches her forehead in confusion. "How will you know when I've captured their flag?"

"Howl," Wolf says, a wicked grin splitting his face.

Charlotte looks like she's about to protest but then a steely determination takes over her face and she gives him a clipped nod before taking off to the left and towards the other team's location.

"Think we should've warned her?" I ask as we watch her disappear into the darkness.

"Nah, she'll be fine."

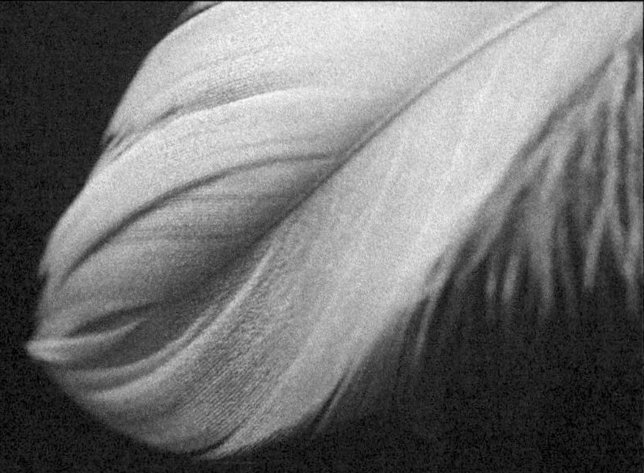

CHAPTER ELEVEN

JAGGER

THE TIPS OF my fingers tingle with a familiar feeling. I allow it to wash over me, more welcoming to the sensation this time than in decades past. Ever since that fateful day that we were cast down to Earth, I've grown to hate the gift that was bestowed upon me. What was supposed to be a gift turned out to be the ultimate curse in the hands of The

Elders. We've been their secret weapons for decades and it's finally time to break our binds.

"The Lamb is roaming free," Kane's voice says.

The one thing The Elders weren't able to bind to their wishes was the ability for the four of us to communicate. Although we suspect they don't know this little tidbit, because if they did when they bound our powers to them, they would've tried to take this too.

Time to see how well the Little Lamb screams.

CHAPTER TWELVE

ARLO

I CAN BARELY SEE a foot in front of me. If I held my hand up in front of my face right now, I doubt I'd be able to see a little more than the outline. The further I ventured into the woods the less light shone down from the moon. It's eerie and at the same time exhilarating. My breathing seems louder in my own ears with the lack of city noise. Every once in a while, an owl will hoot from somewhere in the trees above me. Not often, but just enough to have my heart rate spike again and remind me that I'm not thc only thing in these woods; human or animal. I use my hands to guide me along what must be a hiking trial. The trees here are spaced further apart, far enough that when I lift both arms to the side my fingertips barely scrape along two trunks.

Something snaps behind me and I instinctively duck down. Wondering if Wolf and Kane were able to distract Hunter and Jagger like planned. I strain my ears to see if I can hear anything else beyond the sound of crickets, but there's nothing. I push back up to stand and brace a palm on the tree trunk close by, pausing again to listen. Half expecting some creep in a hockey mask and a chainsaw to jump out right in front of me. When I still don't hear anything, I roll my eyes at myself.

"I need to lay off the horror movies." The fact that I just combined horror movies is enough evidence of that.

I take a couple more steps forward when something brushes against my leg and I'm overcome with an uncontrollable rage. My blood sings through my veins as my fingers curl into fists and dig into my palms. The urge to punch something, to see blood spill is overwhelming, but as quickly as it came the feeling is gone. I stumble back against a tree trunk, palm pressed against my chest, and try to take a deep breath. I've never felt anything like that before. I very rarely ever gotten mad to the point of wanting to hurt somebody, but just then I don't know if I would've been able to control myself from throwing a couple punches if the opportunity had presented itself.

When I'm sure the feeling is completely gone, I start back toward the clearing. My stomach grumbles but I shake it off and keep walking. After another couple steps, sharp pains ping through my stomach. They're so painful that they bring me to my knees in the middle of the forest floor. I clutch my middle in an attempt to alleviate some of the pain, but I'm so hungry. It feels like I haven't eaten in months, which rationally I know isn't true because we just finished having dinner maybe less than an hour ago, but the pain in my stomach has me questioning what is real. I can see the other team's makeshift flag from here, though, and the thought of letting down my team is enough for me to try and fight through the pain. I struggle back to my feet, but stay awkwardly curled in on myself with an arm still clutched close to my belly. After a few more steps the pain recedes and I breathe a sigh of relief. It's quick lived, though, because just before I'm able to clear the tree line and snatch the flag, a figure steps in my path. They're covered head to toe in black, even their face is covered by a black mask. If it weren't for the little bit of light coming down through the clearing, I doubt I would've been able to tell there was someone there until I walked right into them.

"Wolf?" I ask, thinking that maybe it's one of the guys on my team coming to help me, but the figure doesn't move. The hairs on the back of my neck start to prickle and stand up. "Kane?" This time my voice doesn't come out as strong as it did. When the person still doesn't move, my frustration begins to build and I clench my fists causing my nails to dig painfully into my palms. "This isn't fucking funny," I seethe. The person moves then. Just a simple tilt of the head. I'm about to push passed them and continue into the clearing, ready for this stupid game to be over with when the little bit of light catches on something gripped in their hand.

Freaked the fuck out and not wanting to stick around to find out if the knife's fake or not, I turn tail and book it to the left and off the beaten path. Running with my hands up to protect my face from the overgrown branches. I'm too busy looking back over my shoulder to try and see if the person followed me that I don't immediately notice a piece of root from one of the trees sticking out of the ground. My foot gets caught under it and I flail as I barely have time to shoot my hands out in front of me before face planting hard on the other side. I look back at the sound of running footsteps behind me and scramble up to my feet, wincing at the sting in my palms. The running feet are too close now for me to get away. I use my hands to feel around the trunk of a bigger tree and slide down the other side of it, pulling my knees up into my chest and folding my arms around them. Trying to make myself as small as possible. Maybe they won't find me. My breathing sounds so loud in the quiet night. My heart beat like a deafening bass in my ears.

I hear whoever it is, run a little way passed my hiding spot and then stops. I bury my face further into the space between my knees and chest and pray they don't find me while trying to slow my breathing. Where's everyone else? I thought Jules said that we were the only ones up here. If that's true then does that mean that one of them is the one chasing me? And why? I haven't known any of them for long but what reason would they have for chasing me through the forest at night with a knife? *Isn't that how every horror movie starts?* I push the thought aside. This isn't some B-rated horror movie. Taking a chance, I uncurl my arms and peek around the tree half expecting to be met with the sight of the blade, but when there's nothing except trees and bushes, I sink back against the one at my back for a second before pushing up and circling around the other side. Before fully abandoning my hiding spot, I take another look around again. *Where the hell did they go?* When nothing jumps out at me, I take in a deep breath and slowly let it out, convinced that it was just one of the guys playing a prank, and then start to pick my way back to the clearing.

A twig snaps from somewhere close by and I freeze, swallowing hard. Too afraid of turning around and seeing the person with the knife, even though I can *feel* them against my back. I can feel their fingers trace down my spine. I squeeze my eyes shut. I should scream, run, do something, but my feet feel like lead weights. And then it's like my wind pipe is being squeezed from the inside.

I reach up to try to pull whatever it is off but my fingers don't connect with anything. There's nothing physically around my neck and yet I know it's not my imagination. I cough and wheeze as I claw at my own throat and fall to my knees again.

"Please," I wheeze, falling to my side and rolling onto my back, my fingers still trying to claw the invisible grip from around my neck but my limbs are growing weak and my vision is starting to dim. I can barely make out the silhouette of a person standing above me, head tilted to the side. I reach my hand out even though I know the effort is useless. My eyes start to flutter. It's too much effort to keep them open now. I can feel the life draining from my body.

"Arlo!" A voice shouts in the distance followed by more.

"Maybe she went back to the cabin?"

I don't know how long I lay in the middle of the forest floor but it feels like a lifetime before the sound of curses and multiple running footsteps grow closer. I look again to where the person was standing but there's nothing there. This time when my eyes flutter closed, they don't open again.

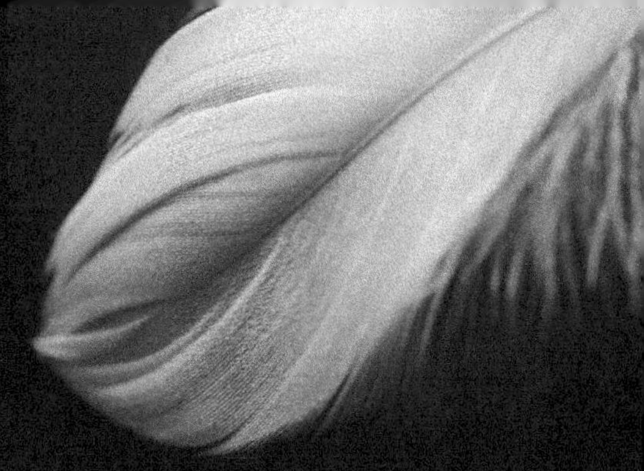

CHAPTER THIRTEEN

ARLO

MY HEAD IS pounding so bad it feels like there's a jack hammer inside my brain. I force my eyes open and immediately shut them, wincing at the sudden stream of sunlight through the drawn-up blinds.

"Oh, thank God!"

At the exhaled words, I turn on my side – earning me a slight reprieve from the light – and see Jules curled up on a chair in the corner of the room. She unfolds her legs from under her and throws the blanket covering them over the back of the chair before crossing the room and sitting on the side of the bed.

"How are you feeling?"

I shrug, scooting up into a sitting position with my back against the headboard. "I've been better. What happened?" I ask.

Jules narrows her eyes. "I don't know. Kane and Hunter went to go find the other guys when you hadn't shown to try and get the flag. I told them it was a bad idea to have left you alone in those woods," she pauses and shakes her. "Anyway, when none of us had found you and you didn't howl like Wolf told you too, we all went looking. Jagger found you first."

I wring my hands in my lap. Everything from last night is a little hazy, but there's something clawing at the edges of my memory, something that I know is supposed to be important. I look down at the chipped nail polish on my thumbs and try to recall what happened after I split from the guys.

"I-I don't remember."

Jules reaches out and covers my hands with one of her own. "It's okay. We'll figure it out." She smiles and I feel some of the tension ease out of my body. "You're probably starving. You slept like eighteen hours. We put a plate aside for you from lunch so come down when you're ready," she says, giving my hands a quick squeeze and then pulling the door part way closed behind her when she leaves.

Gingerly, I throw back the covers and climb out of bed. Physically, I feel fine; no bruises or broken bones so at least that's good, but every quick movement has my head feeling like it's too heavy for my body. I shuffle over to the shopping bags in the corner with some personal items Kane took me to get on the way up to the cabin yesterday, and locate the shampoo and conditioner along with the shower gel and head to the bathroom. I remember Jules saying that the main bathroom upstairs is always stocked with fresh towels so I grab a navy one from the cabinet and start the shower.

I braid my hair in a long French braid after toweling off and getting dressed in a pair of cut off jean shorts and off the shoulder slouchy sweater. I don't feel like doing my make up so I forgo it and head downstairs. As soon as my feet hit the last couple steps, noises from the kitchen draw me up short, but curiosity gets the better of me and I poke my head around the corner. My breath hitching at the scene I almost walked in on.

Kane groans, tilting his head back as Wolf licks up the side of his neck and nips at his earlobe. Kane's fingers curl into the belt loops of Wolf's jeans and tugs him closer. Wolf forces a knee between Kane's legs while his hands slide down to Kane's round ass and he pulls him closer. My belly tightens and the space between my thighs ache. What would it be like to be in the middle of that sandwich? I sink my teeth into my bottom lip to stop from moaning out loud at the picture. Thankfully, the door off the kitchen opens and Jagger and Hunter step inside from the deck. My heart stops, remembering the sounds of Wolf and Jagger together at the party on Friday night. Oh god, is Jagger going to be pissed? What the hell was Wolf thinking cheating on his boyfriend when he was just outside? My stomach drops when Jagger steps closer to Wolf and I get ready to make my presence known and step inside. Hopefully, they won't fight with an audience, but then I stop. Jagger grips Wolf around the back of the neck and then slams his lips down on Wolf's. Hunter steps around to the other side of them and takes over the job of trailing open-mouthed kisses along Kane's neck and jaw while sliding a hand down his abdomen to the front of his pants. When Jagger and Wolf come up for air, Hunter grabs the front of Wolf's shirt and pulls him into a hungry kiss while Jagger devours Kane's mouth.

I swallow hard and clench my thighs together. The sounds they're making are better than any porn.

The door opens again. This time Jules steps through with a plate in one hand. As soon as she sees the guys making out, she groans.

"Seriously? You can't go one whole day?"

Hunter pulls away from Wolf, both of their lips wet and kiss swollen. "No." He grins.

Jules rolls her eyes. "But really though, I don't want to see my brother making out or getting his dick sucked." She shivers, going over to the fridge and pulling something out. "Plus, we have company."

I take that as my cue to back up some and then make a bit more noise before turning the corner and entering the kitchen. All heads turn in my direction and I can feel my cheeks immediately heat. I can't even look the four of them in the eyes without thinking about what I saw just moments ago. So, I'm relieved when Jules tells me to take a seat at the kitchen table and that she'll reheat the lunch I missed a few hours ago. The kitchen and dining room is an open concept so I'm not entirely closed off from the stares I can feel boring into my back as I make my way around the kitchen island and over to the long pine table.

Jules brings over my plate and I thank her before taking a bite of the hot dog. I must have been hungrier than I thought because in no time I've finished the hot dog and Caesar salad. My stomach still grumbles so I push away from the table with the intent of making another hot dog but I pause just as I'm about to turn towards the kitchen. Four sets of eyes are staring at me. As well as four identical smirks. Hunter not so subtly elbows Jagger in the ribs who then clears his throat and takes off for the front door with the other guys following behind. Oookay, so that was weird.

"Here," Kane says, reaching out for my plate. His fingers brushing mine. "You relax. I'll make you another one. Ketchup and mustard?"

Still confused, I nod and then slowly sink back down onto the bench seat. I rest my elbow on the table and prop my chin on my palm, watching Kane move around the country style kitchen. His movements are graceful and fluid. The muscles of his biceps contract and release with each movement and it's a valiant effort to tear my eyes away from the vein porn.

"So, um, what's the plan for today? Are we heading back?" I ask, desperate for a distraction.

Kane places the plate in front of me and then straddles the bench seat so that he's facing me. He leans on his hands between his legs and I can't help but stare at his arms. They really are impressive. Especially when he's flexing them like he is and the veins are popping.

"We were thinking we'd take it easy today. Maybe watch a movie, make some pizza, and then head back late. We all got an email earlier from Mac saying that class was cancelled tomorrow so we don't have to be back til late."

I reach for the napkins in the middle of the table and wipe my hands off after devouring that last hot dog. When I turn back to Kane, there's a playful grin curling his lips.

"What?" I ask.

His grin grows as he slides the napkin from between my fingers and then begins to lean in. My breath hitches and my heart starts beating a frantic rhythm with how close he is. I would only need to lean in a few inches to close the distance and have his lips on mine. Kane gently wipes the corner of my lips with the napkin and heat creeps up my cheeks. Of course, I have ketchup or mustard on my face. I expect him to move away again and put some distance between us, but he crumbles the dirty napkin in his fist and pinches my chin between his thumb and forefinger. My eyes dart down to his mouth and I lick my lips remembering him making out with Wolf and then Hunter and *dear God…* and then Jagger.

It feels like years have passed but really, it's only been a matter of seconds before the little bit of distance between us disappears and his lips are closing in on mine. Then his hands are on my hips. I gasp as he maneuvers me into his lap. Kane uses the opportunity to lick into my mouth and I whimper, wrapping my arms around his shoulders and pulling myself closer against his body. His hands roam my back and then one slides up to grip the back of my neck. I vaguely wonder if any of the flavours I'm tasting on his tongue are from the other guys. He tastes like chocolate, cinnamon, caramel, and coffee. His mouth is like a fucking dessert and I'm ravenous, but there's something else too. Something that's all him. One of his hands roams up under my shirt and I shiver, loving the feeling of his rough hands against the smoothness of my skin.

Kane groans when I rock my hips forward and over the erection tenting his sweatpants. Thank you, God, for inventing sweatpants. The thought is like a bucket of cold water when I remember Hunter's hand disappearing under the waistband of Kane's sweatpants not even half an hour ago. Wrenching my lips away from his is painful, but I somehow manage to do it and then scramble off his lap.

"Oh god. I'm so sorry. That—"

"Was fucking hot," Kane says, palming the front of his pants. He chuckles, "You're drooling, Little Lamb."

I snap my mouth closed and then swallow the pool of saliva. "We shouldn't have done that. You're with them." I wave my hand in the general direction the other three went. "And I'm not a home wrecker."

Kane tilts his head in confusion and then understanding. Like a wild cat stalking its prey, he pushes up from the table and slowly advances on me. With every step he takes, I take one back until I'm being pressed up against the wall. He takes my chin again and forces my eyes up to his. "Were you spying on us, Little Lamb?" He tsks.

"I… what? No," I stammer and then huff, trying to look away but he forces my face back to him.

He takes another step closer, forcing a knee between my legs and pressing closer until there's zero space left between us. I can feel every hard edge of him. "Did it turn you on?" He says, his breath warm across my cheek as he leans down close to my ear. "Did you wish it were you in the middle instead of me?" He trails his fingers down the center of the V of my shirt. "Were you imagining all four of us surrounding you? Our mouths tasting your creamy skin? Our hands exploring." He nips at my jaw and I shiver, losing the battle with my self-control and gripping his hips.

"Kane," I moan, tilting my head to the side to give him better access to my neck.

He wastes no time and soon his tongue is licking a trail from my collarbone to just below my ear. The same as what Wolf had done to him not too long ago. I want to touch him. I need to feel him under my fingers. I slide my hands from his hips to around his back and under the hem of his black t-shirt. He groans, resting his forehead against mine and punches his hips forward causing his hard cock to rub against my thigh.

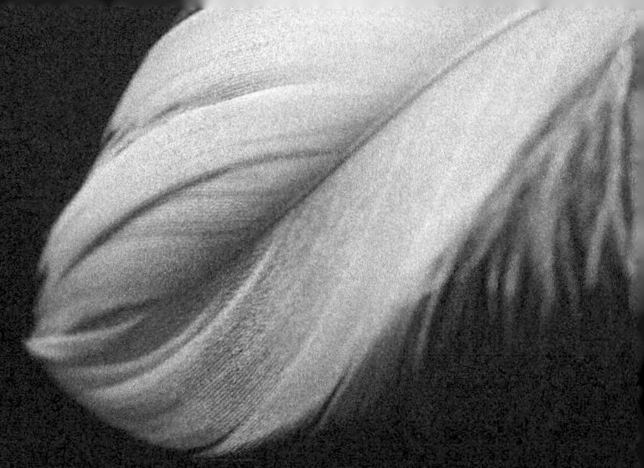

CHAPTER FOURTEEN

WOLF

"WHERE THE HELL'S Kane?" Hunter grumbles, lofting Jules suitcases into his vehicle.

Apparently, the answer to how many suitcases one chick needs for a night in the woods is a fuck ton. Hunter's trunk is filled with her cases with only a small opening in the side for his and Jagger's duffel bags.

I shrug, carrying my own bags to Kane's SUV and dropping them by one of the back tires. "I thought he was right behind us. I'll go see what the hold up is," I say, trudging back to the cabin.

We're planning on leaving later this evening after dinner, but Hunter wanted all the bags packed and vehicles loaded up early so that we just have to jump in and head out. Except, nobody can get into Kane's car to put the coolers in the back because he has the keys. The scene I walk in on in the kitchen has me wishing not for the first time that Jules wasn't here with us because god damn. I quickly and quietly pull my phone out of my jeans pocket and snap a picture — thankfully, I still have the sound off — and send it to the other guys through the group chat. My phone pings almost instantly.

Jagger: Fuck me running sideways.

Me: We could just send Jules back in an Uber.

Hunter: Don't be a dick.

Jagger: I agree.

Jagger: With sending her in an Uber. Or she can take Hunter's car and the rest of us can cram into Kane's.

I have to admit, Jagger's idea has merit. Kane's SUV is bigger than Hunter's Jaguar. The five of us can fit comfortably in the Jeep. Or our Little Lamb could sit on my lap. I grin and reach down to press a palm against my hardening erection. Yeah, I have no qualms with that at all. Having her round ass in my lap for however many hours it takes us to get back to the house.

Arlo moaning Kane's name snaps me out of my day dream. As much as I would love to continue this little show, Kane's stepsister is still somewhere in this house and while she's okay with catching the four of us in random states of undress, I'm not sure how well she would react to this.

Clearing my throat, I cross my arms over my chest and lean a shoulder against the door frame.

"As hot as this is to watch, we have cars to load up."

When horror at being caught in a compromising position crosses Arlo's face, I want to kick myself. Maybe I could've had more tact in letting them know I was there, but then Kane whispers something in her ear and she immediately relaxes. Her body melting into his. Lucky fucker.

Arlo slumps against the wall when Kane pulls away. Both of their lips swollen and wet. My dick jumps at the sight and I'm seconds away from pulling them both into my arms and tasting their lips. Kane slaps me on the shoulder on his way out to the front. As soon as he's gone, Arlo straightens up from the wall and turns to me, sucking her bottom lip between her teeth and looking at me from under long, black lashes.

"You okay, Little Lamb?"

My question startles her and for a second, she stares at me with wide grey eyes, but then she blinks shyly and nods. "Yeah. I'm okay."

I step closer to her and using the side of my index finger, tip her chin up. “What did Kane tell you just then?”

Her bottom lip is back between her teeth and I want to groan. What I wouldn’t give to taste that lip.

“He, uh…” she pauses, her eyes darting to the side before coming back to rest on mine. “He said that I could be in the middle… of the four of you. If I wanted.”

Fuck yes.

I let my gaze slide down to her lips and fuck me if she doesn’t part them. “And do you?”

“I-I don’t know.”

That gets my attention and I glance back up at her. She shrugs but doesn’t make a move to step back.

“This is all too confusing. I just met you all a week ago, and yet I feel like…”

“You feel like what?” I ask when she trails off and is silent for a while.

Her pale grey eyes roam my face and settle on my lips before making eye contact again. She steps closer, putting a hand on my chest. "I feel like I know you. All four of you. I already feel comfortable around you which is weird because this weekend is the first time all week that we've exchanged more than just a couple words." She stops to take a breath but her other hand keeps flailing like it's saying all the words her mouth can't. Even while she digs the pads of the fingers of her other hand into my chest. Her eyes are frantic. "This is crazy, right?"

I cup her face in one hand and rub my thumb over her bottom lip. The flesh slightly catching under the pad of my thumb. "Take a breath, Little Lamb." I grin when she glares up at me. "Who said crazy is a bad thing? Normal and safe are boring," I add. "Plus, do you want to say that you lived your life by other people's expectations or that you lived unabandoned?"

She sighs, resting her forehead beside the hand on my chest. "You're right."

"C'mon." I take the hand from my chest and bring it up to my lips to press a kiss to the back. “Let’s find Jules so we can pick a movie and get the pizzas started.”

CHAPTER FIFTEEN

JAGGER

SEEING ARLO ALL snuggled up and cozy between Wolf and Kane has me feeling some kind of way. Nothing bad. It just proves what we've kind of known from the first day we saw her. This weekend has sealed it for us. She belongs with us. I only wish that Hunter and I were sitting with them too. But the four of us agreed not to crowd her and let her get used to two of us first. The four of us together can be a bit overwhelming. Not long after we began preparing the toppings for the pizzas, Jules got a call from her roommate saying that the apartment above theirs had flooded and there was some water damage coming down the wall into their apartment. So, she had to hightail it back to Toronto. I'm still not entirely convinced that one of the other guys had nothing to do with it, but I'm also not about to look a gift horseman in the mouth.

Feeling a little left out, I shift onto my hands and knees and crawl up Hunter's body where he's laying sprawled on the second couch beside me. I fit myself into his side with my back against the back cushions and slide a leg between his. His blue-green eyes blaze with heat when he glances down at me and quirks a brow. I shrug and then grin, reaching behind him and pulling a blanket from the back of the couch down and over us. I hear Wolf or Kane chuckle from their own couch but I don't pay them any attention. Kane's stepsister walked into the kitchen before I had a chance to get my dick sucked earlier and I have a major case of blue balls after the intense make-out session that was interrupted.

Just thinking about it has my dick perking up. I slide a hand down the front of my pants and adjust myself, whimpering when I remove my hand and my dick rubs up against Hunter's leg. With my head resting on his chest, I trail a hand down the center of his chest under the blanket and then finger the waistband of his sleep pants where the head of his cock peeks out.

Hunter's palm lands against my ass cheek with a swat. I suck in a breath at the quick jolt of pain and peek up to see Wolf, Arlo, and Kane watching us. Arlo is a bright shade of red and it's sexy as fuck. Makes me wonder if the rest of her turns the same shade. When she notices us looking at her, she quickly turns away and back to the movie playing on the big screen. I can't even tell you what we're watching, the need to grind against Hunter and spill my load is the only thing I can concentrate on. He groans into the top of my head and shifts his legs open a bit wider when I get my fist around his thick length after pulling his pants down to below his balls. My hips punch forward and my eyes roll in to the back of my head with the friction. But it's not enough. Hunter growls low when I release my hold on his cock to undo and shimmy my own pants down.

"Someone's impatient," I tease.

"Horny," he grunts like some fucking caveman which only makes my dick get harder. He stiffens and then breathes out a long breath before whispering in my ear. "Go to my bedroom. Strip and get on the bed on your hands and knees and wait for me."

I inhale a shuddering breath while burying my nose in the side of his neck and just nod. Reluctantly, I pull my pants up again, careful not to brush the material against my dick and then climb off of Hunter. Since Jules had to leave early, we all decided to stay an extra night seeing as how our early morning class for tomorrow was cancelled. The guys and I don't have a lecture until two in the afternoon. But Arlo has to be back for a Psychology lecture at ten. So, it's not unusual when I tell them I'm going to hit the hay since we have to be up early to make sure Arlo gets back in time. Even though, I don't for a second believe that they really think I'm heading to bed.

Once I get to Hunter's room, I do what he said and strip. Piling my clothes on the chair in the corner. I pull out a condom and lube from one of the night stands and toss them on the bed before getting on my hands and knees in the middle of the king-size mattress. We all got queens when we purchased the place, but Hunter had to be extra and go for the King. It's also part of the reason why eighty percent of the time when we're up at the cabin, we all pile into Hunter's bed.

I hear the click of the door as it opens and then closes again, but it's almost a full minute before the bed dips behind me and Hunter's palms are roaming over my ass. He pushes them apart and then without warning, his tongue is right there too; licking a strip over my hole.

"Jesus, Mary and Joseph." My back bows and I grip the sheets on either side of my head.

Hunter doesn't acknowledge my near heavenly gasp. He keeps on eating my hole like he's starved and it's his favourite meal.

"Hunter," I moan, pressing my forehead into the pillow.

He hums against my hole and then a finger is replacing his tongue. He shifts behind me and peppers sucking kisses first, up my spine and then all over my back. By the time he enters two fingers inside me, I'm a writhing, mumbling mess.

"Don't make me beg, asshole," I grunt when he pegs my prostate again.

I can feel his lips tip up in a grin against the side of my neck. "But you're fucking sexy when you beg. When you're close to tears that all you can do is hold on for the ride."

“Kinky fucker,” I say on another moan. I whine at the empty feeling when he removes his fingers, but he doesn’t wait too long before the head of his cock is right there, pushing passed the tight ring of muscle. “Yes. Yes. Fuck Yes.”

The bastard chuckles, banding an arm around my chest and pulling me up so my back is flat against his chest. He nips my earlobe, giving it a sharp tug. The sharp sting mixes with the pleasure of his dick brushing against that magical spot inside me. I’m so close. I take my leaking dick in my hand, gathering the pre-cum from the tip and using it as lube. I work my fist up and down my length, twisting on the upstroke over the crown. I drop my head back against Hunter’s shoulder and let it loll to the side, giving him easier access to lick and suck my neck which he takes full advantage of.

With an arm still around my chest, he grips my hip in his other hand and squeezes as his thrusts speed up. I match the speed of my fist around my dick with his and soon I'm right there, balancing on the edge.

"Hunter," I groan, desperate for the release I was denied earlier. Desperate for more.

"I've got you."

He releases me, pushing me down on my face with my ass still in the air. Hunter gets up on his feet and mounts me, keeping a hand on the middle of my back. This new angle has me seeing stars and my head spinning. I feel like I'm drowning with no possibility of a life raft. This thing with The Elders has taken its toll on all of us over the last several years. Taking our frustrations out on each other's bodies is just one very effective way of alleviating the stress and uncertainty.

"Come for me, Jagger. I want to feel your hole clench around my cock." His voice is rough and commanding, and it's exactly what I need to let go and let the waves over take me. I sink my teeth into the fabric of the pillow to stifle my scream as thick ropes of cum shoot from my dick.

Hunter's thrusts stutter and then he's coming. I can feel his cock pulsating as he empties into the condom.

Unable to keep my own body weight up off the bed after he's removed the condom, I let my knees slide from under me. Ignoring the cooling puddle of cum I'm lying in. My body too sated and my mind too at rest for me to give a shit right now. I don't even hear Hunter go into the attached bathroom to dispose of the condom. My eyes drift close and I barely notice being rolled over and something wet and warm wiping over my abdomen before sleep pulls me under.

CHAPTER SIXTEEN

ARLO

I'M STILL EXHAUSTED when the guys drop me off at my apartment just before nine a.m. I have approximately an hour before I have to be ass-in-chair in my Intro to Psych lecture. I hate this class with a passion. I don't know how people find this stuff interesting. To me it's just a snooze fest. I wish I could skip it, but we're the second week into the semester and if I start skipping classes now, it'll set a bad precedent for the rest of the semester. No, I'll just have to suck it up and deal. Maybe I'll sit in the front today and see if that'll help keep my attention from wandering, but I doubt it. Especially after this past weekend.

What a weekend.

I was not expecting any of that to happen, but I'm not mad it did. I just wish my memory of the night of the capture the flag game wasn't so hazy. Whenever I think about being in the forest behind the cabin, a niggling happens at the back of my head like there's something important about the events of that night that I need to remember. It's frustratingly annoying. This is the first big gap in my memories that I've experienced.

Except for the night your dad died.

I immediately push that thought aside. My dad died when I was six and he wasn't even on the same continent when his life was taken.

Are you sure? There's a reason why you keep having the same reoccurring dream, Charlotte.

I want to tell the voice in my head to shut up because she doesn't know what she's talking about. Mom would never lie about how my dad was killed. Although… she has been pretty tight lipped about him in general ever since he passed. I shake my head and dump the shopping bags full of items the guys bought me this weekend on the bed before grabbing clean clothes and underwear from my dresser and head for the shower in the main bathroom.

Twenty minutes later, I'm busy blow drying my hair into sleek, straight locks when my roommate pushes open my bedroom door.

"Sorry, didn't think you'd hear me if I knocked."

I hit the button on the blow dryer to turn it off and then turn my attention to Morgan. "That's fine. What's up?"

She shrugs, but the movement is stiff and so not like her. "I noticed you didn't come home last night or the night before. Everything okay with your mom?"

"Everything's fine. I actually had to cancel our weekly dinner dates," I say. "I went to Jules' cabin for a couple nights."

Morgan's eyes widen and something unrecognizable flashes behind them, but then she blinks and it's gone. She's relaxed again. "That's cool," she says, taking a seat on the foot of my bed and leaning back on a palm. "Anyone else go besides the two of you?"

Usually I wouldn't hesitate to tell the truth, but for some reason I want to keep what happened up at the cabin between me and the guys. I mean, it's weird, though, right? Having a crush on four guys who also happen to be friends and sleeping with each other. Making out with two of them was weird enough and I felt like complete crap about it. But then I remembered what Kane said and suddenly I didn't feel like crap anymore. I was… turned on. The possibility that my shower daydream could possibly be a reality was a really hot thought. At least for as long as we were secluded in that cabin, but the minute we entered the Toronto city limits, it was like a bucket of cold realization. Even if, for some unfathomable reason, the five of us were together, no one – and I mean *no one* – would understand. The world still struggles with accepting LGBTQ+ couples. Minds would explode if the five of us came out as a couple. Wait, couples? A quintilople? No, that sounds weird. I push the thought aside for now and quickly think of something to tell Morgan.

"There were a bunch of us," I say, eventually. It's not a lie, but it also doesn't give away anything.

She stares at me unblinking, her head cocked to the side. I try not to squirm in my chair, but there's something off about the way she's looking at me. It makes me slightly uncomfortable.

"Jules' stepbrother and his friends weren't there?" Her eyes narrow into slits, watching my reaction.

I was slightly uncomfortable until now. Now I'm suspicious and suddenly feeling protective over the guys.

"No." The lie comes surprisingly easy. I just hope my poker face is up to par. "I need to finish getting ready and head to class soon," I say, holding up the hair dryer.

"Oh, yeah. Sorry." She smiles but it doesn't reach her eyes and then she climbs off my bed and leaves, pulling my bedroom door closed again behind her.

Something about the whole interaction doesn't sit well with me but I don't have time to contemplate it right now. I finish blow drying my hair and apply the barest of makeup before pulling on a pair of ripped skinny jeans, a black graphic tee and my leather jacket. I slip on my heeled motorcycle boots at the door before grabbing my backpack, wallet, and keys and leaving the apartment. On the way down in the elevator I pray it's not a day of tons of walking because these boots are new. I cringe remembering the last time I decided to break in a brand new pair of boots and then ventured downtown for the day. I can still feel the ghost pain of the blisters from that day.

I make to it my Psych 101 class with five minutes to spare so I unpack my laptop and get it set up. Ten a.m. comes and goes with no sign of the Prof, and when ten minutes pass and then twenty, students around me start packing up their stuff and leaving, and I happily follow their lead since I wasn't really keen on it today anyway. I follow the herd of freshman students down the three flights of stairs and out of the Arts building before venturing right to the path that winds passed the gym and to the large football field. I spot an overgrown tree at the far side along the fence and make my way towards it, dropping my backpack against the trunk and dropping down on my butt.

Minutes later, the football team runs out onto the field and starts running laps around the track on the far side. It doesn't take me long to spot Jagger in the lineup. He's not as built as a couple guys on the team, but he's fast. Faster than the others. My face flushes when I remember the way he groaned as Hunter's hand slipped under the blanket when the two of them were cuddling on the couch together last night. I figured all of them were the dominate types in bed, but Jagger submitted without any hesitation to Hunter last night. It was hot as fuck to witness and made me wish that I could've been on the other side of their bedroom door. Not necessarily to participate, at least not at first, but to watch. I groan, thankfully no one is around and the team is too far away to hear. Jagger and Hunter together would be hot as fuck. Hunter is taller and broader than Jagger. He's rougher too – physically. Where Wolf has the rugged biker look going on, Hunter is pure CEO. Kane reminds me of an MMA fighter, and Jagger is the ball player.

When the team splits in two and lines up at the line of scrimmage, I pull my head phones from the side pocket of my backpack and plug them into the port of my phone then scroll through the Spotify app until I find the album I've been obsessed over. As Jake Scott's voice croons through the earbuds, I lean my head back against the tree and close my eyes, allowing the music to lull me into a sense of calm.

CHAPTER SEVENTEEN

JAGGER

“MARTINEZ! GET YOUR head in the game!” Coach yells when I fail to block a play… *again*.

Fucking hell.

I can’t concentrate knowing that Arlo is sitting under a tree looking like sin in that biker getup. It makes me hard seeing her in that leather jacket and those ass kicking boots. I spotted her the minute we ran out onto the field and I've had one eye on her ever since. Which means only half of my attention is actually in practice. We line up at the line of scrimmage again. This time I manage to block a couple plays before Coach blows the whistle and calls practice done. I grab my duffel bag and slip away before he has a chance to ream my ass out. I know I need to be better and get my head in the game. We have a game coming up against UofT. We need to win this one if we want to get ahead and stay ahead for a chance at the playoffs at the end of the season.

Arlo still hasn't noticed me when I drop my bag next to hers and drop down on the other side of her. I pluck an earbud out of her ear and bring it mine, leaning my head on her shoulder so not to pull the other bud out of her other ear. She startles, her eyes flying open until she sees its just me and then relaxes again.

"You scared the crap out of me, Jagger."

I chuckle. "Sorry, Little Lamb. You should've been paying more attention to your surroundings."

When I got closer and realized that she couldn't hear me because she had earbuds in her ears and her eyes closed, white hot anger burned through my veins at the thought of someone else walking up to her and Arlo not noticing until it was too late. Just because it's a university campus doesn't mean shit. A lot of bad stuff has happened on a campus. I mean, I had an eye on her but I was across the field and also half not paying attention. Who knows how long it would've been until I realized that something was wrong? And what if I didn't have enough time to get to her? I try to push the thought away and reassure myself that she's okay and unharmed. Nothing happened.

"Who's this?" I ask, meaning the artist singing.

"Jake Scott. I haven't been able to stop listening to this album on repeat."

"I like it," I hum, curling an arm around her middle and settling in.

"Jagger," she huffs. "You're all sweaty and we can't take a nap in the middle of a school day."

"Why not?" I ask, already half a sleep. After the first round with Hunter last night, I woke up after about an hour and wanted to go again. We eventually fell asleep around five and then were up at six getting the cabin cleaned up before hitting the road. I'm exhausted and Arlo makes a comfy pillow.

"Jagger." She pushes on my shoulder but I don't budge. "Jagger!" she says again, this time louder.

"I'll get up," I pause. "Only if you agree to go back to my place and take a nap." I tilt my face up to her and grin.

Her grey eyes look almost blue as she glares down at me, but then her lips slowly curl into a smile that makes them sparkle and I have to will my dick to stay down. She chews on her lip a bit before answering. "Okay, fine. Deal."

I immediately jump up and offer my hand for her to take. I throw my duffel bag over my shoulder and then pick up Arlo's backpack, ignoring her when she reaches out a hand to take it from me. Instead, I clasp her outstretched hand in mine and intertwine our fingers. She quirks a questioning brow but doesn't say anything as I begin walking us to the TTC station. Once we're on the train, I go back to leaning my head on her shoulder and Arlo hands me one of the earbuds. I can get used to this. When I'm with her, the jumbled mess in my brain quiets down. My body doesn't feel as wound up, and I can actually relax.

Soon we're at our stop and I get her hand in mine again as we emerge up on the street and ten minutes later, we're walking through the front door. I kick off my shoes in the entryway and head up the stairs with Arlo following close behind. As soon as I enter my bedroom, I strip off my shirt and workout shorts then climb into bed, holding the covers up for her to join me. I probably should've showered or at least rinsed off before getting into bed, but all I can think about right now is falling asleep with Arlo's body wrapped around mine. I'll wash the sheets later. She peels out of her tight jeans but leaves her t-shirt on as she crawls in beside me and immediately curls up on my side, intertwining her legs with mine and laying her head on my chest, her hand resting on my hip.

"Jagger?" Her voice sounds small in the big room.

"Hm?"

"You're all sweaty." Her lips curve up as she smiles against my chest. She giggles when I reach under her arm to tickle her, but fuck, the way she curls in closer to me. It does something funny to my chest.

"Tell me something about yourself that nobody else knows?" I ask when our laughter dies down.

"I took last year off to go cage diving with sharks." The way she says it, is so nonchalant that for a moment I don't believe her.

"Wait, really?"

She nods against my chest. "I've had a love for sharks for as long as I can remember. Growing up, my entire bedroom was decked out in all thing's sharks. Where most girls my age were obsessed with the Bratz Dollz or Barbie or whatever, I was obsessed with sharks and dinosaurs." She giggles. "I had to convince my mom to let me watch Jurassic Park when I was five because I wanted to see all the dinosaurs."

"And did she let you?"

"No," she sighs, drawing little figures on my chest with the pad of her finger. "My dad ended up convincing her to let me watch it. He promised if I got nightmares from it that he would stay up with me." Her voice is no longer the happy, carefree one it was minutes ago. Instead there's a sadness underlining it, but I'm not going to push and ask her about it if she's not ready to talk.

"Did you get nightmares?" I ask, gently squeezing her against my side in an offer of comfort before letting her go again.

She chuckles. "Nope. If anything, I was too wired to sleep. I knew there two more movies and I wanted to watch them all that night. Eventually, dad said we could have a marathon the next weekend if I kept my room clean. I think my room was the cleanest that week than it ever was."

"What about Jaws?"

Arlo groans and buries her face in my neck. "I *did* get nightmares from that movie but I think it was more the theme song that caused them, than anything." She laughs. "Deep Blue Sea was actually the movie that solidified my love of all things sharks. Even as a kid I knew that what they were doing to those sharks was wrong. A part of me always thought that I'd go into marine biology."

"Why aren't you?"

She shrugs in my arms. "I would have to move to a coastal town to do any co-op or internship term, and I don't know if I can be that far away from my mom. It's always just been the two of us since my dad died. I'd feel guilty if I just upped and left for several months or a couple years."

I pull her closer into me and kiss the top of her head. "If it's been your dream then I'm sure she'll understand, Little Lamb."

"Yeah, maybe."

There's a lull in conversation as we both digest it, but it's not uncomfortable. It's… nice. Eventually, I doze off with Arlo snuggled up against me.

CHAPTER EIGHTEEN

ARLO

I LEFT BEFORE JAGGER woke up. He looked so peaceful in his sleep that I didn't want to disturb him so I snuck out as quietly as I could and sent him a text letting him know that I didn't want to wake him. We slept for much longer than either of us planned too because the sun is just about fully set when I run into Kane walking up the front walk of their house.

He gives me a knowing smirk but doesn't say anything about my sleep rumbled appearance. Even if he had asked, nothing happened with Jagger. After agreeing to have lunch with them on campus tomorrow, I start to head back towards the TTC station when Kane calls out to me.

"Let me drive you. It's late and who knows what kinda creeps are on the train at this hour."

I turn around to face him, but keep walking backwards, lifting my hands in a shrug. "I'll be fine."

"Charlotte," he growls. "Get in the Jeep."

He opens the passenger side door and motions for me to get in, but I just grin, wave and turn back around. I've walked the streets downtown numerous times at night over the last week and nothing's happened. I'm sure I'll be fine, but it's nice to know that someone, other than my mom, cares whether I make it back safely or not. However, by the time I make it to the end of the street and turn the corner

I'm rethinking whether I should've just accepted the ride. It's not completely dark yet, but it's past the time when the street lights should've turned on. However, all of them are out except the one at the end of the block. It's the last corner I need to take before reaching the train station. Shivers race up my spine – and not the good kind. I pull my leather jacket tighter around me and put one foot in front of the other.

Street lights go out all the time. There's nothing to worry about. There's plenty of time left before it gets really dark out. Plus, Kane is just around the corner. If I scream loud enough, he'll come running, right? Right!

I am such an idiot, but the closer I make it to the end of the next block without something happening, the more I start to relax and laugh at myself. That is until someone dressed in all black steps out of an alleyway between two houses. I scream and jump back two spaces, pressing a hand over my chest above my racing heart. The man just stands there, staring at me. Head cocked to the side. At least I'm assuming it's a guy with the baggy clothes and hoodie pulled up over his face. But the way he's looking at me forces a memory that I had forgotten.

When the person still doesn't move, my frustration begins to build and I clench my fists causing my nails to dig painfully into my palms. "This isn't fucking funny," I seethe. The person does move then. Just a simple tilt of the head. I'm about to push passed them and continue into the clearing, ready for this stupid game to be over with, when the little bit of light catches on something gripped in their hand.

My eyes dart down first to his right hand and then his left. That's when I see the same blade as that night up at the cabin. This time I scream bloody murder and turn around to bolt back to the house the guys share and where I left Kane and Jagger, but a strong hand curls around my upper arm and turns me around while shoving me up against a rock wall and covering my mouth with the hand not currently holding the blade of a knife to my throat. I'm close to hyperventilating while clutching the arm of the hand holding the knife and praying it doesn't accidentally slip in his hand.

"What do you want?" I sob, squeezing my eyes shut for a second to try and pull myself together before opening them again. The black hoodie is pulled too far down for me to see his face except for his mouth and the stubble lining his jaw.

"Stay away from The Four Horsemen," he says, his voice gravelly, like he swallowed a handful of rocks before jumping me on the street. His lips part again but he snaps them shut when shouting starts from the block I came from. He curses, putting just enough pressure on the blade for the tip to pierce my skin. "If you value your life, you'll stay away from them." And then he's gone.

I crumble to my knees in the middle of the sidewalk and fold my arms around myself. Vaguely aware of voices calling my name, car doors shutting, and then footsteps getting closer.

"Arlo," Jagger says crouching down in front of me and rubbing his hands up and down my arms. "Are you okay?"

Wolf slaps him upside the head. "Dumb question, man. Of course, she isn't okay."

The two of them help me to my feet again and each throw an arm around my shoulders. It's an awkward three-way hug but it's exactly what I need right now. Kane comes running back towards us. He stops in front of us and rests his hands on his knees while he tries to catch his breath.

"He got away." His brows furrow and pull down in the center.

Kane straightens to his full height and takes my chin in his fingers lifting my face up and moving it from side to side before dropping his hold and letting out a string of expletives, some of which I don't even think are in English. He runs a hand through his messy blond hair and then pulls me out of Wolf and Jaggers arms and into his own. My fingers curl into fists around his shirt on their own volition and

I bury my face in his chest, ignoring the sting of the cut along my neck.

After several more seconds, he pulls away and takes my face in his hands. "Let's get you back to the house and cleaned up. You can stay the night with one of us and in the morning, we'll take you back to your apartment."

Too exhausted to argue, I simply nod and follow his lead. We all pile into Wolf's car and he makes a U-turn, heading back toward the house.

"How did you know something was wrong?" I finally ask when he parks on the street out front.

Wolf shrugs, "I didn't. I was on my way home when I saw you on the sidewalk."

"Jagger and I were just starting to head to the train station to make sure you got home safe when we heard you scream," Kane says and Jagger nods.

"I woke up and you weren't in bed with me. Wanted to see where you got off too," he adds.

Once we're all back inside the house, Jagger takes me to the guest bathroom to help clean the cut on my neck while the other two guys search the kitchen for something to eat.

"Can I ask you something?" I say, when I'm perched on the closed toilet lid with my head tilted up so that he can clean the little bit of blood trickling down from the wound.

"Shoot."

I watch him snap off the latex gloves he donned to clean the blood and then rip open a band-aid.

"Why the Four Horsemen?"

Jagger pauses with the band-aid half way to my throat. A shadow passes over his face but he quickly shakes it off and smooths the adhesive down on either side of the wound. "It's a stupid nickname we were given as kids and it stuck."

I may not have known these guys for long, but I can tell when someone's lying and the way Jagger avoids any eye contact and busies himself around the bathroom, straightening things that don't need to be straightened, I can tell he's lying. There's more to it than just a nickname.

Wolf hands me a mug of chamomile tea when Jagger and I emerge from the bathroom and join him and Kane in the living room. We've just settled in to watch an episode of Lucifer before bed when the front door opens and a sweaty Hunter walks in.

"Well, isn't this a nice surprise." He grins, dropping a gym bag in the entrance-way and grabbing a water bottle from the fridge.

"Dinner should be ready in twenty," Kane says.

Hunter drains the bottle before tossing it in the blue recycling bin beside the fridge and then wipes his sweaty forehead on the sleeve of his t-shirt. "Cool. I'm going to hit the shower then." He gives us a mock salute on his way past the couch and up the stairs.

Is he the guy from tonight? He wasn't there when the other three showed up to scare my attacker away. I mentally chastise myself for the thought. There's no way Hunter's involved. What reason would he have to warn me off his friends? Plus, I'm pretty sure he's the type of guy who will come out and say if he didn't want me around rather than play games and try to scare me.

But if it isn't him then who is it?

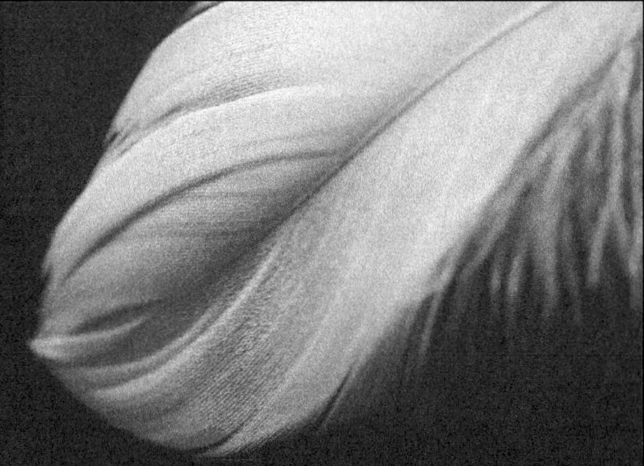

CHAPTER NINETEEN

ARLO

I CRAWLED BACK INTO bed beside Jagger again last night and despite the events of the evening, I slept well. If 'well' means waking up every three hours to the memory of the blade being pressed into my throat and wondering if anyone in the surrounding houses would have come out to save me. Then, yeah, I slept well. My phone alarm goes off on the small table beside the bed and I flail an arm out to turn the annoying sound off.

Jagger's arm curls around my middle and drags me back until I'm pressed against the hard ridges of his front.

"If there's ever someone with a good enough excuse to skip classes today, it's you, Little Lamb," he says, his warm breath ghosting across my ear.

"I'm fine," I reply, and wiggle further back against him. Trying to soak in his warmth.

He groans, tightening the arm around my middle and thrusting his hips forward, dragging his cock along the crease of my ass. My head drops back against his shoulder and I arch my back.

"Arlo," Jagger breathes, a warning in his voice.

I turn onto my other side so that I'm facing him, and cup the side of his face in my palm. "Please, Jagger," I plead. "Make me forget about last night. I just want to feel you."

His green-gold eyes rake over my face and then settle on my lips. I poke my tongue out and lick along my bottom lip, pulling the flesh inside of my mouth and sinking my teeth into it. Jagger groans low and long like the last remnants of his control are obliterated. He mirrors my position and frames the side of my face, using the pad of his thumb to tug my lip from between my teeth and then his lips are there. His tongue licks along the seam of my lips and I open for him easy. I lower to my back and Jagger follows, positioning himself between my legs. I wrap my legs around his waist and rock my hips up.

"Christ." He drops his forehead to the pillow beside my neck, leaving open-mouthed kissing along the curve where my neck meets my shoulder, and rocks his pelvis against mine.

Using my feet, I manage to push his boxers down to just below his ass. Jagger shifts, supporting his weight on one fore-arm, and helps me by pushing down his boxers in the front so that they pool around his knees on the bed. He leans across the other side of the mattress and pulls open the top drawer of the nightstand. Jagger pulls out a condom and leaves the drawer open as his full attention lands back on me.

"Are you sure?"

I nod, pulling my underwear to the side with one hand and using the other to play with my clit. His lids droop to half-mast, his pupils blown with lust when he grips the edge of the foil wrapper between his teeth and rips it open, spitting the wrapper onto the floor beside the bed and rolling the condom down his length. Jagger grips the base of his cock in one hand and lines up the head with my entrance, while his gaze ping pongs between mine like he's making doubly sure that this is really what I want. Frustrated that he's taking so long, I wrap my legs around his hips and slam my hips up, taking his length in one go.

"Fucking hell." His hand moves from the base of his cock to under my thigh and lifts my leg higher and drives deeper inside me.

I moan and claw at his back, dropping my other foot back to the bed and tilting my hips. The change in angle makes his cock brush against that sweet spot and I gasp, pulling him tighter. We're so lost in each other that neither of us hear his bedroom door open and close or are aware that we have an audience until the chair in the corner of the room squeaks. Jagger immediately stops thrusting and I freeze, looking over his shoulder and to the left to see Wolf sitting in the chair, an ankle crossed over his knee and a shit-eating grin plastered across his face. There's no denying the pure lust burning in his eyes, though.

"Please," he says, his voice rough. "Don't stop on my account. I was curious to see what all the noise was about." He winks and Jagger growls, but I can feel his cock give a little twitch inside me. Seems like he likes the idea of being watched.

I take his face in my hands again and force his eyes back down to me and kiss him. "I'm okay with it if you are," I say, when we pull apart.

A wicked grin pulls at his lips. He pinches my chin in his hand and turns my face toward where Wolf is sitting. Jagger runs the tip of his nose up the line of my jaw to below my ear. "You want him to watch me fuck you, Little Lamb? Want him to hear how you're going to scream for me? Want him to see how hard you come on my dick?"

I shiver and groan. Then whisper, "Yes, please."

At my confirmation, Wolf drops his foot to the floor and I can get a clear, unmistakable view of a bulge in the front of his blue basketball shorts. Jagger thrusts hard and fast, and my eyes roll to the back of my head. But then he pauses and looks back at Wolf.

"No touching. Just watching. Unless she says different," he says, and Wolf gives a clipped nod in acceptance.

I hadn't thought of that, so I'm glad that Jagger saw to say something. I mean,

I wouldn't have minded if Wolf did start touching me, but I'm too close to the edge. If I had both of their hands and mouths on me, I would probably die from sensation overload. Jagger pulls out and then flips me onto my stomach, manhandling me until I'm on my hands and knees and facing Wolf in the corner of the room. Then without any warning, Jagger slams back inside me, taking my hips in a bruising grip and thrusting hard and fast. Wolf's eyes flash red for a moment before returning to their usual dark brown. But the change was shocking enough that I'm sure I'm not imagining it. However, when he reaches into his shorts and pulls out his cock, all thoughts of red eyes disappear. I watch him stroke himself with his fist to the thrusts of Jaggers hips behind me and it's all too much. The head of Jagger's cock brushes against my g-spot once… twice… and that's all I need to go careening over the edge.

"Don't you dare fucking muffle it. I want to hear you scream," Jagger demands when I drop my head to bite into the comforter.

Unable to hold it off any longer, I do what he says and don't bother trying to stifle the scream that rips from my throat as waves of pleasure roll through me. From the corner of the room, Wolf curses and drops his back against the chair as ropes of thick cum spurt from the head of cock and land on his sweaty work out shirt. *That was fucking hot.* Jagger's fingers dig harder into my hips, his movements jerky as he, too, comes.

After we all get cleaned up, Wolf climbs into bed with us and I fall asleep cocooned between him and Jagger, wholly unaware of how my life is about to change.

CHAPTER TWENTY

HUNTER

"FUCK YOU GUYS." I hear Kane say to the others as they enter the barn. "I should've been there too." He pouts and I swear, he almost stomps his foot like a toddler. Almost. His face contorts in pain at the amount of restraint it took for him to hold back. For as long I live, I'll never understand why he was chosen as *War*. I have never seen a guy more easily riled up and ready to fight than Kane Davis. Although, maybe that *is* why he was chosen. When he gets riled up for a fight, it seeps out of his pores like a clear, odorless gas, affecting everyone within a 10km radius. Everyone, except for Wolf, Jagger, and I. We're immune to each other's gifts.

Wolf chuckles, snatching Kane up in a headlock and giving him a noogie. "Better luck next time."

Jagger rolls his eyes as he strolls passed the two trying to wrestle each other and leans against a wooden post beside where I'm standing, propping a booted foot up behind him. "Where've you been the last couple nights?"

I shrug, tucking my phone back into the inside pocket of my jacket. "Busy." I glance at the two juveniles and sigh while scratching the back of my neck. I hate nights like tonight, but they've been a necessary evil for as long as we've been stuck down here. And they'll continue to be unless we can find a way to undo the curse The Elders placed on us.

"Halloween is in six weeks," I inform them when Wolf and Kane have joined us.

"Fuck. Already? Didn't it just happen?" Kane says, running a hand through his hair. He hasn't shaved it in a few weeks so it lost its military style. This new style suits him though.

Jagger snorts. "It happens every year at the same time."

Kane glares at him and folds his arms across his chest. "I'm aware of that. I was just—" He pauses, looking around the empty barn before continuing. "Wishing it would be different this year."

"We all did," Wolf adds, solemnly.

"She can't be here when it happens," I say, knowing we're all thinking it but none of the others are willing to speak it out loud.

"The fuck she can't." Wolf puffs out his chest and clenches his fists at his sides like he's getting ready for a fight, and I can't exactly say that I wouldn't welcome the distraction and the pain right now.

Three pairs of eyes glow red as they each turn to stare at me. I hold my hands up, palms out, in front of me. "I didn't say I liked it, but you all know as well as I do that if we ever have a chance of reversing whatever the hell was done to us then, Charlotte Williams cannot be in Toronto when the clock ticks over into October 31st. It's the one night a year when they see everything."

"Isn't that even more of a reason to keep her close? How are we supposed to reverse anything if we can't fucking see them?"

It's not that we can't literally see them, we can. But when The Elders bound our gifts to themselves there was an unseen consequence. Every year on October 31st, when the veil between the paranormal world and the real world is down, they are able to see and hear our every thought. They're able to see what matters most to us and just how much we're willing to give up to protect it. Because of this, they cannot know about Charlotte. At least not until we're ready for them to know. If they find out about her before then, who knows what they will do. Our gifts are permanently tied to us, the curse only allows The Elders to bind themselves to our gifts and our immortality temporarily. Every year, it needs to be redone unless they can find a way to separate the gifts from our souls, for lack of a better word. Hopefully we will have found a way to reverse the curse and destroy them before that time comes.

"Maybe we should just call Hades," Jagger suggests.

"No," I snap.

Kane grins mischievously. "Scared to see your ex? How long has it been now? A hundred years?"

Ignoring him, I say, "We'll do it ourselves. The last thing we need is for the world to figure out that all the myths they were told as kids are real." I may still be a little pissed that my ex is the reason why I was 'blessed' with the gift of *Death.*

Not that taking a life can't be fun, but it wouldn't have been my first choice. My phone pings and we all collectively hold our breaths as I pull it out to check the message. "It's go time," I say, motioning for Wolf and Kane to open the stall and uncage our latest prey.

They drag him out of the stall by his bound wrists. Jagger and I follow but stop and wait further back while they untie his hands and rejoin us. The man turns around in circles a few times until he realizes that his hands are free. He rips the blindfold from his face and does another half circle, coming to a stop in front of us. We've already put our masks in place and pulled down our hoodies so he can't see our faces. Wolf starts off our chant like he's always done over the last century.

"Do you want to play a game?" Jagger's voice rings clear in the night surrounding the barn and cabin further up the hill.

"Is this some sick joke?" The man now in the middle of our circle says, spinning around to try and keep us all in his line of sight.

"We'll even give you a head start," Kane adds, his voice dead.

Before the words fully leave Kane's lips, the man darts for the tree line and disappears from sight, and not a moment too soon. I start to feel the familiar tingle begin to race up my back and down my arms to the tips of my fingers. I bring my hand up to my face and twist my wrist back and forth, reveling in the power again for however long we're allowed to this time. From the corner of my eye I see Kane jumping up and down, working his shoulders back and forth. Red sparks zap all over his body, eventually accumulating around his hands and disappearing under his skin like his body is sucking in as much of the power as it can because it never knows when the next time will be. I turn toward the others and see the same thing. Jagger's sparks are black and Wolf's are blue. The same blue our… I shake off the thought before it has time to take root and work my neck side to side, until I hear the satisfying crack.

As one well-oiled unit, we take off for the forest at the same time. Wolf veers off to the left and Jagger to the right with Kane and I taking point in the middle. We slow our steps, ignoring the natural sounds of the woods at night and instead focus on the sound of running steps and panted breath in the distance. Our prey is running out of steam and fast. Probably because, unlike the others, he didn't stick to the hiking trails. Unless you know where you're going, the terrain in these woods isn't very forgiving unless you stick to the worn in foot paths. A howl sounds in the distance, close to where I assume our prey is. Kane snickers beside me.

"Do you have to do that every-goddamn-time?" I grumble.

"You're just jealous," Wolf says back.

"Ow! Fuck!" Comes Jagger's voice.

Wolf laughs. *"What the fuck did you do?"*

"Stubbed my fucking toe on a root."

I can't help it. I snort.

"So you're saying your night vision sucks as much as your regular vision."

Kane shoots me a grin over his shoulder and holds up a hand for a high-five. I don't leave him hanging and slap our palms together.

"Fuck you too, jackass. Can we please focus and find this asshole? I forgot how much these woods suck at night. Fuck I'm out of shape."

"Says the university football player," Kane taunts.

"Found him." Wolf's voice breaks through the back and forth chatter between Kane and Jagger. *"This guy reeks of piss and fear."*

Wolf howls again and soon we're crowding in on our prey from all directions. I don't remember how we decided who would go first in torturing our prey before we put them out of their misery, but it was an unspoken agreement that Jagger would go first. Making them feel so hungry that all they can do is curl up in a ball and sob until the pain in their stomach subsides. Most of them prayed for death because they couldn't handle the hunger pains. This man refuses to even whimper. Next up is Wolf. He draws a finger down the man's cheek, instantly making him break out into a cold sweat as his temperature spikes. *Finally, a reaction.* He starts gasping for breath and lifts a hand from his side to reach for Wolf, but he's too weak to lift it more than a couple inches off the ground.

Wolf and Jagger go back and forth. Alternating bestowing their gifts on the man as Kane and I stand back and watch, waiting for our turn. Just before the man can give up and give in to the call of letting go of his life, they stop and take a couple steps back, giving him room to breathe before Kane steps up. He pauses and looks to each of us first, waiting for our nods of readiness, and then leans down and helps the man to his feet. The change happens as soon as he's upright. The defeated and scared look he wore only moments ago is replaced with one of rage. I feel the corner of my lips curl into a half smirk as I watch him snarl at us while clenching and unclenching his fists. The material of his dress shirt is ripped and dirt stained from being dragged across the forest floor but he doesn't seem to notice or care. The need to fight and inflict violence is outweighing everything else to him right now. He makes a move toward Jagger first, throwing his entire body into the right hook which Jagger manages to side step with ease.

He grunts but comes back swinging at the first person he sees, which just so happens to be me. He throws another punch which I block and then drop into a crouch, swinging my leg out and kicking his out from under him. Sending him falling to his ass. He hits the back of his head on the ground when he lands and lays there in a daze for a second before pushing to his feet again and brushing off the leaves that have clung to his once pristine navy suit. I'll give the guy credit. He might be a stuck-up suit who thinks he can get away with robbing people of their hard-earned money and murder, but he's put up more of a fight than some of the street thugs we've hunted.

Kane lands a jab to the man's ribs, forcing him to curl in on himself while stumbling back a few steps. Wolf turns a questioning look on me.

"How much longer you plan on dragging this out for? We can't chance him making a run for it."

"He's right, H," Kane chimes in. *"Guy's tougher than he looks in that damn suit."*

I honestly hadn't expected to drag it on for as long as it has but we've all needed something to take our frustrations out on tonight. Two birds, right? I crouch down in front of where he's now lying sprawled out on his back. Jagger almost put his lights out with that last hit. He might be the smallest of the four of us, but he's just as strong, if not stronger. I cock my head to the side while I take in the extent of the man's injuries and try to determine the best cause of death.

There's bruising all over his face and body. There's a cut below his one eye and I think his lip is split. It's hard to tell with the stream of blood spilling out the side of his mouth and blood running down from his nose. I sigh and drop my chin to my chest while resting my forearms on my knees. We really did a number on this one.

"You already get his wallet and stuff?" I ask Wolf.

"Before we left the barn."

He steps up closer and crouches down beside me, taking a hold of the man's ankles and using his gift to make him weak so he won't struggle as hard against what I'm about to do as if he wasn't subdued. Jagger and Kane pin each one of his arms down as extra precaution.

"Sean Grahame, The Elders have found you guilty of crimes of racketeering and murder, and hereby sentence you to death."

Pale electricity sparks from my fingers as I hover my hand, palm down, over his heart for several seconds before slamming it down over his flesh. I can feel the tingles seep out from my fingers down into his heart. He gasps, back bowing up off the ground and struggles against the hold the other three have on him. Soon it's over and he slumps back to the ground, his lifeless eyes staring up at the opening through the trees at the bright night sky.

Just like every other time before, I take out my phone and shoot off another message. I've lost count of what number we're up to now as far as bodies are concerned, but hopefully Sean will be the first of the last.

CHAPTER TWENTY-ONE

ARLO

THE FIRST WEEK of October hits with a biting cold. Signalling that it's no longer summer, and fall has officially arrived. I fold one of my many knitted infinity scarves around my neck and grab my backpack before heading out the door for campus. We have a midterm in our Mythologies class so I don't get to talk to the guys in the lecture hall. The exam is mostly made up of multiple-choice questions and I'm not even mad at it. I would take hundreds of multiple-choice questions over essay or short answer. Those are the bane of my existence. Mostly because I can never seem to get my brain to come up with answers that aren't a bunch of gibberish and will actually make sense.

There's one question near the end that captures my attention and makes me pause more than any of the others, and I don't have a good explanation as to why.

Who were the Four Horsemen of the Apocalypse?

a. Zeus, Artemus, Hera, Poseidon

b. War, Famine, Plague, Death

c. God, Jesus, Mary, John.

I circle B and then flip the booklet back to the beginning before gathering my stuff and taking my completed exam to the front. I place it in the already growing pile and then exit the class. Hunter is leaning against a row of lockers when I turn the corner, hands jammed into the front pockets of his wranglers, booted foot propped up behind him. With Jagger and Kane standing on either side of him.

"Wolf still writing?" I ask. I can't remember if I saw him when I left.

Jagger is the first to notice me standing in front of them. He grins, throwing an arm around my shoulders and pulling me into his side. I melt into him as my face flushes with memories of that night a couple weeks ago. We haven't slept together since, and not from lack of trying either. But every time we make plans to get together, he either gets called away or Mom makes last minute plans with me. I feel so guilty for bailing on her that one Sunday that every time she calls to make plans I immediately agree. I know I shouldn't still feel that way weeks later, but she's all I have.

"Wolf isn't the best test taker. He'll be out in a minute, though," Kane says, pushing away from the lockers and stepping close to me. He frames my face in his palms, not caring that Jagger still has his arm around me and leans in close. "Hi."

He's so close, his lips brush against mine with a feather light touch at the word.

Then he's kissing me for real and I can't help but chase his mouth when he leans away and breaks the kiss. Hunter chuckles from where he's still leaned up against the lockers but then he gets this look in his eye that I can't quite make out. He abandons his spot holding up the wall of lockers and then he's the one kissing me. My head spins and I feel dizzy. Hunter tastes like a caramel Werther's candy.

"Mm," he hums, brushing a thumb back and forth over my cheek bone. "I've been wanting to do that for a while now."

Someone lets out a dreamy sigh nearby and I think it might be me. That's the first time Hunter's kissed me and my brain is having a bit of trouble catching on to the fact that Hunter Anderson just kissed me. A throat clears and I automatically jump back from Hunter, pressing close to Jagger again. Wolf watches us with a… well, a wolfish grin plastered on his face.

"Well, that was certainly a treat after that hellish exam."

Kane slaps a hand on Wolf's back and then throws an arm around his shoulder, bringing him in for a bro hug. "Awe, you jealous, bro?"

"Fuck off," Wolf grumbles, playfully pushing Kane away.

Kane grins then snatches a hand around Wolf's neck and hauls him in for a hot as fuck kiss. Wolf pulls him close, their bodies aligning like they were made for each other. I don't think I'll ever get used to seeing them make out with each other. Even though, they seem to always be touching or kissing whenever they can. When they finally come up for air, Kane's mouth and chin are red and angry from Wolf's beard, but he doesn't seem to care when he pulls Wolf in for another kiss. Just a peck this time. Something weird happens to Kane's eyes when they pull apart again. His normally whiskey-coloured eyes are… red? I watch as Hunter pulls Kane down to whisper something in his ear. Kane squeezes his eyes shut and when he opens them again, they're their usual colour. When I look around the group, nobody has seemed to notice the sudden change. Assuming that it's all in my head, I hook a finger in the back pocket of Jagger's jeans and snuggle closer into his side.

When the different classes start letting out into the hallway, the guys decide to walk me to my next class across campus. A month into classes and it's still hard for me to believe that I'm here. I don't know how many nights I stayed awake dreaming of the day I would be able to attend Queen's University. There was this calling that I could never quite seem to describe when Mom asked me why Queen's and not Ryerson or York. But there was this feeling of rightness, and that feeling only grew when I stepped foot on the campus that first day back in September. But it solidified when I met the guys. I don't understand why, but there's something about this campus and the four of them that makes me feel like this is where I'm supposed to be. After years of feeling like I don't belong, like I'm the odd one out, I finally feel like I'm… home.

We're learning about Maslow's Hierarchy in Intro to Psych today, so I open my laptop and tune out the majority of the lecture. Only tuning back in when the Prof throws up a quiz question on the projector. Maslow's Hierarchy of needs was something I learned back in high school during a social studies class. Nothing has changed between the material I learned then to what we're learning today. I pull up Bing in Safari and start researching for my final paper in my mythologies class. Mac gave us three broad topics at the beginning of class that we can choose to write our final research paper on. Greek Mythology, Roman Mythology, and Christian Mythology. I start researching potential topics within Greek Mythology since that seems to be the most popular one. But the longer I scroll through pages and pages of academic articles on Zeus, Hades and Athena, the more I begin to lose interest. A lot of students in the class will probably be choosing Greek Mythology because it's so popular. I need something that will stand apart from the rest. In the first lecture, Mac had mentioned bonus marks for the paper that shows the most originality in terms of topic. I click over to the University's academic research article database and on a whim type in *The Four Horsemen of the Apocalypse*. The hairs on the back of neck stand up as I read through the first article. There's something about the horsemen in the bible and my four guys that makes goosebumps pebble down my arms. I get lost in the biblical literature surrounding the Four Horsemen and Revelations, and before I know it the rest of the class is packing up and heading for the doors.

I head across the football field to the gym where Kane mentioned he booked some time in the ring. I pull open the heavy metal door and have to squint against the darkness until my eyes adjust to the low light. Kane is in the far corner of the boxing ring with his back to me. My eyes roam down the length of his back and the way the muscles in his shoulders pull and release as he tapes up his hand. When he moves to tape the other, red sparks shoot out the tips of his fingers. Kane startles and then closes his fist, digging the pads of his fingers into his palm before releasing it again. The sparks are gone. I'm not entirely sure if I made a noise but Kane looks over his shoulder, shock clear in his whiskey eyes before his face relaxes into the boyish smile I've come to know as pure Kane Davis.

"Hey, Little Lamb. Been there long?"

I glance down at his fingers but they look normal. No red sparks of electricity. "Um." I shake my head and start again, hiking my backpack up higher on my shoulder and stroll toward him. "No. Not long. Are you just getting started?"

"Why? You looking for a show?" He grins, leaning his arms on the top rope.

I roll my eyes but return his grin. "And if I was?"

Kane tilts his head to the side, studying me for a minute before he steps back from the rope and bends down to pry apart the middle two ropes.

"Get your sexy little ass in here."

"What?" I squeak, looking around the gym, but nobody else is in here with us. "Aren't you waiting for someone?"

"Nah. Now get in here."

With a reluctant sigh, I drop my back-pack to the floor beside the ring. My leather jacket follows and I kick off my boots.

"I'm not dressed for this," I say, once I'm in the ring and facing him.

"Real life isn't going to wait for you to be properly dressed. It's better to train in your everyday clothes. That way it becomes more second nature and you'll be able to react on instinct."

Makes sense. I take a deep breath and let it out slowly. "Okay, so now what?"

"So now you're going to try and block me. Keep your hands up to protect your face." He takes hold of my wrists and pulls my hands up so they're in front of my face. "Don't ever close your fist over your thumb. That's the fastest way to break it, and trust me, it hurts like a bitch."

Kane swings at me and I try to lift my left arm in time to block his fist but I'm not fast enough and he clips me on the chin. Not hard, but enough that I feel it. He moves a few steps back, giving me time to recover and telling me to stay on the balls of my feet.

"If you're constantly moving, it'll be easier to block the attack," he says.

When I nod to give him the green light, he advances, forcing me to move backwards around the ring. Kane doesn't stop moving, he keeps bouncing on the balls of his feet while moving in circles to try and find an opening. This time when he swings his left fist low towards my ribs, I'm faster and able to block the blow.

"Good. Now, I'm going to try and grab you. When I do, bring your hands up to my shoulder and use my momentum to pull me forward and down and bring your knee up." I must look constipated because Kane chuckles then says, "relax. You got this."

He lunges at me like he said he would and I try to concentrate on his instructions and do exactly what he said, but I don't want to hurt him so when I bring my knee up, I slow my movement, barely tapping the top of my knee against his stomach. When I let him go, Kane backs up again.

"Arlo." There's a slight growl to his voice when he says my name.

"What?"

"You're not going to break me."

"I don't want to hurt you," I say, my voice more like a whisper in the big room.

"You won't." He backs me into a corner, gripping my chin between his fingers and tugging my bottom lip from between my teeth. I wasn't even aware that I had started chewing on it. "Do you trust me?"

I gave him my sweetest smile, while trying to subtly hook my foot behind his ankle without him knowing. I curl my fists into the front of his shirt, running my tongue along my bruised bottom lip while looking up at him from under my long lashes. Kane's breath hitches and his nose flairs. When he moves to grip my hips, I give him a playful shove backwards. He flails before hooking an arm around my waist and pulling me down with him. I land on his chest with an oomph, my legs on either side of his and our bodies perfectly lined up. Kane grips the nape of my neck and pulls my face down to his, kissing me like we're the only two people left in this world. I lean up on my knees and sink down until I'm sitting on him. His cock twitches behind the material of his gym shorts and I moan, grinding down on his length and seeking out the friction I crave.

Kane's hands slide up my jean clad legs and under my shirt to my waist. His rough, calloused hands are a stark contrast against my smooth skin, but they feel good. He pulls me down for another kiss. One hand reaching up to cup my breast over my bra and the other keeping hold at the back of my neck. I mirror him. Sliding a hand around the back of his neck to tangle in the newly grown out hair there while my other, curls around the fabric of his muscle tee. I rock my hips, working my core back and forth over his growing erection.

"Christ, Woman. You're trying to kill me," he pants when we finally come up for air.

I mewl, rubbing on him like a cat and press my lips to the curve of his neck, right in the middle of his tattoo. "Please, Kane." I loosen my grip on his shirt and trail it down his middle to the waistband of his shorts. Slipping a finger under the band, I drag it back and forth over his belly.

Kane snatches my wrist in his fist and halts my movements. "Little Lamb, don't play if you're not ready for the consequences."

CHAPTER TWENTY-TWO

KANE

HER GREY EYES grow wide and there's a fire that sparks behind them at my words. My dick gives another twitch. Arlo's eyes drift shut like she's in heaven as she grinds harder against me. Frustrated with all the clothes between us, I grab hold of her shirt at the neck and rip it in two, then flip us over until she's on her back underneath me. I lift one of her legs and wrap it around my waist, rolling my hips down at the same time. Arlo arches her back. The long line of her neck, exposed to my taking, and I fucking take. I drop down, making sure to keep the majority of my weight supported on my forearm planted by her head, and run my tongue up the line of her throat.

"Kane."

My name is like a breathless purr from her lips. She fingers the hem of my shirt and I lean up only long enough for her to pull the material off before resuming my position between her thighs. Arlo locks her ankles behind my back and then rolls us again until she's the one on top. She braces her hands on my chest and then drops open-mouthed kisses down the center of my abs, raking her nails down my body as she goes. Her tongue dips into my belly button and then licks a stripe down until it gets cut off by my shorts. She pouts, and god damn, that's the sexiest thing ever. Arlo curls her fingers in the waistband of my shorts and tugs them down along with my boxers. I lift my hips and then help her get rid of the offending clothing by kicking them off. When she gets her first real look at my cock, her pink tongue peeks out and licks along her lips.

"Fuck me, I'm going to come before I even get inside you if you keep doing that."

Arlo grins mischievously and does it again. I growl, launching up and grabbing her behind her neck, hauling her mouth down on mine as I roll us again and pin her beneath me.

"What did I say about playing with me, Little Lamb?" With one hand around her throat, I undo the button on her jeans with the other and rip the zipper down.

She nibbles on her bottom lip, her eyes hazy with lust when she replies, "That I better be ready for the consequences."

Fuuuck. The way her voice takes on this sweet, innocent quality is my undoing. I remove my hand from her throat, and yank down her jeans and underwear in one go, not bothering with pulling it off her ankles. In fact, I use the pants to lift her legs high in the air, exposing all of her to me. Her pussy is already glistening for me, ready for its punishment. But I still can't stop myself from sliding two fingers into her tight heat. Arlo moans, pushing her head back into the hard mat of the boxing ring, arching her back, and forcing my fingers deeper. *Christ.* I curl my fingers and try to find that spongy spot that I know will drive her wild. As soon as I do, she begins muttering incoherently, her hips bucking up against my wrist.

Arlo whimpers in protest when I remove my fingers but as soon as I replace them with the head of cock and begin pushing inside her, she moans low in her throat and claws at my back, pulling me down to her. At some point she must have kicked her jeans off from around her ankles. She's so fucking beautiful with her dark brown hair spread out like a dark halo around her head. Her grey eyes, drooped to half-mast and dark with lust. Her lips kiss swollen. I tug down one side of her bra and lick around her pink nipple. She shivers under me and hugs me tighter. I keep my thrusts slow but deep, not wanting this to end too soon, but knowing that if we don't hurry up, we will get caught. The same thought must have dawned on her too because she wraps her legs back around my waist and lifts her hips up to meet each one of my thrusts. When she throws her head back and screams, I hurriedly kiss her, swallowing all her delicious sounds. When we do this again, I'll make sure she'll be able to scream as loud as her little heart wants. The walls of her pussy squeeze around my cock as she comes, sinking her teeth into the curve of my neck.

I'm right there. I can feel it but I can't reach it. I pick up my thrusts, going harder, faster. Arlo skims a hand down my back and dips a finger down my crack. I freeze up for a brief second before groaning. The sound of my balls slapping against her ass echo around the large room but neither one of us seems to care right now. Arlo circles a finger around my hole and before she can push the tip inside, I'm coming.

I drop down on top of her, careful to not give her my full weight, as spasms rack my body from probably the most intense orgasm I've had in a really long time. I bury my face in her neck and place a gentle kiss right below her ear. When I lean up so I can see her face, there's a blissed-out smile pulling at her lips. She looks close to passing out and all I want to do is pull her into my arms and fall asleep holding her. But then she frowns and reaches a hand up to trace a finger along my eyebrow.

"Kane, your eyes..." She trails off, cocking her head to the side.

"Hm?" I start leaning into her again, desperate to inhale her scent. Especially now that she smells like lavender, sex, and me.

"Your eyes are red."

That gives me pause. I turn my head to look in the mirror across the gym. Sure enough, my eyes are glowing the same red they do when we hunt. When Arlo starts to follow my gaze, I quickly shut my eyes, praying that when I open them again, they'll be normal.

"Kane, are you alright?"

"Yeah." I clear my throat from the rocks that suddenly decided to take residence. "I'm fine. Probably just tired. We should get you cleaned up and then get out of here before the wrestling team comes in."

Arlo winces when I pull out. I grab my shirt from where we threw it across the ring and then clean her up first before cleaning my cock. I hand her my sweater when her shirt slips through her fingers in a torn and tattered mess.

"That was my favourite shirt," she grumbles, zipping up the blue hoodie. She's swimming in the damn thing, but seeing her in my clothes does something funny to my chest.

I pull her in to a side hug and kiss the top of her head. "I'll buy you a hundred more," I say, and she giggles.

We manage to leave the gym without being caught and go in search of the others.

CHAPTER TWENTY-THREE

ARLO

I FEEL LIKE THE shittiest friend in the history of friendships. Kane called this morning and said that they wouldn't be able to meet up until late tonight. Something about their parents being in town. I didn't quite understand the voicemail message he left, but I also got it a couple hours after he left it so I didn't want to call him back and interrupt the time he was spending with his family. Which is why I didn't even think about texting Jules. I just assumed she was part of said family. Until my phone pings from the living room with a new message. I pull the spatula from the cake batter I was mixing and lick off my fingers before fetching my phone. I head back into the kitchen while opening Julie's message.

Jules: Howdy stranger. You home?

Me: Howdy?

Me: Have you been binge watching country western movies again?

Jules: Maybe. I wouldn't have been if someone wasn't ignoring me *crying emoji*

Me: I'm sorry.

Me: Aren't you going with Kane to see your stepdad today?

Jules: I wasn't invited.

Jules: Open the door

Frowning, I place my phone face down on the counter and go to open the front door. Jules is leaning a shoulder against the adjacent wall, phone between her hands. At the sound of the door opening, she looks up and pops the gum in her mouth.

"I'm starving. Let's go to that new burger joint down the street."

I roll my eyes and step aside to let her in.

"Hello to you too."

She grins, sashaying into the apartment. "Hi," she replies. "So? Dinner?"

"Yeah, sure why not." I hurry to my bedroom to grab my purse and keys.

"Does Morgan want to come?" Jules asks when I come back to the kitchen to get my phone.

I shrug. "I don't even know if she's home."

I head to the front door without bothering to check if Morgan's in her room or not. She's been asking a lot of questions about the guys whenever we're home together recently and it's starting to grate on my nerves. I lock the door behind us and we take the elevator down to the lobby before stepping out into the chilly mid-October air. I shiver and pull my leather jacket tighter around me. I freaking hate winter.

Since I have no idea where we're going, I follow Jules' lead up the sidewalk. Dodging men and women in suits just getting off work and university students heading home from late afternoon classes. Ten minutes later, we stop in front of a black brick building with huge windows and golden lights strung up along the top and down the sides. We step up to the counter and put in our orders before grabbing the table numbers and going in search of somewhere to sit.

Jules heads to a bar height table near the front window and I follow her. Choosing the seat beside her so that we can both people watch.

"I'm sorry," I say after a few seconds of silence.

Jules turns to look at me over her shoulder. Hurt clearly visible in her blue eyes. She shrugs. "It's okay. People have always wanted to get close to Kane."

Crap, is that really what she thinks? That I would only want to be friends with her to get close to her stepbrother? *What did you really expect? You haven't exactly made an effort to hang out with her in almost a month.* I sigh. It's a wonder that she's still talking to me.

"It wasn't intentional, but it doesn't make what I did to you any less wrong. I'm sorry. I should've been a better friend to you this month."

Jules smiles around the straw in her milkshake. "You're forgiven."

I start to relax at that, until her smile grows into something more playful.

"On one condition," she adds and I groan which makes her giggle. "Go dancing with me this weekend. Doesn't have to be tonight. There's this new club that opened up a few weeks ago and I've been dying to go try it out."

I perk up at that. I haven't been to a club since I turned nineteen the summer before school started. Plus, it'll be Thanksgiving weekend. The school gives us Friday (which is today) and Monday off. "Okay, deal," I say and then take a drink of my milkshake, wincing against the brain freeze of drinking too much too fast.

Jules does a little dance, punching her arms up and down in the air above her head. A few passerby's give her a weird look but they keep going. All except one. A bright grin spreads across Morgan's face when she spots us and hurries a little way down the side walk to the main door of the restaurant.

"Hey ladies," she greets us, bright grin still planted firmly on her face as she drops her shopping bags in the seat across from Jules and jumps on the one beside me. Morgan is a little on the shorter side at 5'3 so it's a struggle for her to hop up on the bar height chair.

"Hey, how's it going? We were going to invite you to dinner but you weren't home," Jules replies.

I can't exactly fault her for wanting to include Morgan, hell it would be nice to have another girl friend, but there's something about her that still doesn't sit right with me. Maybe it's just in my head. I internally shrug and shift in my seat so that my back isn't to Morgan. Just then our waiter brings Jules and I our food and takes Morgan's drink order. She already ate so she doesn't order food.

"So," she says when Jules and I have taken the first bites of our burgers. "Your brother and his friends aren't hanging with you guys tonight?"

"Nope. Just Arlo and I tonight." Jules grins around a mouthful of hamburger. "I'm trying to convince her to go dancing at that new club with me."

Morgan's eyes light up and she sits up straighter. Appearing completely invested in Jules' plan. "Oh! That's a great idea! I went during opening weekend. It was so much fun. You should invite the guys too and, uh… their girlfriends."

The bite of burger I just bit off feels like rubber going down my throat when I swallow. Out of the corner of my eye I see Jules' lips twitch but it's nothing more than a minuscule movement. She puts her half-eaten burger back on the plate and picks up a napkin. "No girlfriends as far as I know." She shrugs. "But they're Kane's friends so you'd have to ask them if any of them are single."

I have to dig my fingers into my thighs under the table to keep me from launching myself at Morgan and wrapping my fingers around her neck. I excuse myself to go to the bathroom and pull my phone out of my back pocket as soon as I've locked the stall door.

Me: Question

Kane: Might have an answer

Me: How hard would it be to hide a body in the city?

Jagger: What the fuck?

Wolf: Not hard.

Hunter: I'll get the shovel.

Their responses make me laugh out loud before I can think about stomping it down.

Jagger: Okay, before we go balls to the wall on this whole hiding the body

thing. First, who are we killing and second, did they hurt you? Cause if they did, I'm with Hunter. I'll get the garbage bags and zip ties.

Wolf: I've got the weights.

I roll my eyes and quickly type back a response.

Me: Slow your rolls. It was a hypothetical question.

Hunter: And we gave you a hypothetical answer *wink emoji*

Kane: What's going on, Little Lamb?

Me: My roommate. She showed up at the restaurant Jules and I are having dinner at. She asked Jules if any of you are single.

Those three little dots appear and disappear four times. Four. Times. Two minutes goes by without them reappearing again. I sigh, sliding the phone back into my pocket and flushing the toilet before unlocking the door and washing my hands at the trough-like sink. It's stupid that I feel this weird claim towards them. We're not anything. We're just having fun passing the time since we're all single. Right? So why then does it feel like I want to go all She Hulk, gather them to me and proclaim them as mine? They still haven't replied by the time I've dried my hands and heading back to the table where Jules and Morgan seem to have gotten cozy in my absence. Jules throws her head back and laughs while Morgan giggles at something she said.

"Hey," Jules says when I take my seat again. "You okay?"

"Yeah, why wouldn't I be?" I ask, refilling my milkshake from the tin they bring you.

"You were gone for a while we were starting to worry."

I shrug. "There was a line up," I lie, sipping my drink a little slower this time. That brain freeze really hurt. I sit back and listen to them continue their conversation about the management class they're both taking. When I feel my phone vibrate against my ass, I'm almost relieved for the distraction. I pull it out to find a text from Kane in the group chat with the other guys.

Kane: Where you at?

Me: The new burger place on 42nd. Bin4.

There's no response for a few minutes so I place the phone face down next to my plate and continue munching on my fries. These things are so good. I try to tune into Jules and Morgan's conversation again but they're talking about business stuff that I have no idea about so I tune out and pick up my phone, swiping until I get the Vegas Slots game. I should probably make some kind of effort to try and understand what they're talking about, but it's been a long week and frankly I'm mentally exhausted. A few more minutes pass by before a white Range Rover peels into a parking spot right in front of where we're sitting. I can vaguely make out the shapes of two people in the front seat. When all four doors open and the guys step out, I feel my shoulders instantly relax. Jules and Morgan haven't noticed them yet so I take the extra time to watch as Wolf pulls open the door and gestures for the other three to enter ahead of him. Hunter says something to the host whose eyes crinkle in the corners when he laughs. He points to our table and Hunter slaps him on the back on his way passed. The other guys following. As soon as they round the table, they greet Jules and I with hugs, but the moment they turn to introduce themselves to my roommate, they freeze.

"Hello, boys," Morgan says, her voice a little to breathy for my liking. She's smiling at them like she already knows them. And hell, maybe she does. Queen's is a big school with lots of different classes. It's possible that she's in one of their other classes, but I don't think so. Not with the way she's looking at them like she just discovered a secret they've been harbouring. And them? They all look like they've seen a ghost.

When Jules and I had finished our dinner, the guys offered to drive us home. Although, I think it was more a demand and less of a suggestion. We drop Morgan off first and I decide to go for the drive and spend more time with the four of them since I haven't seen them much the last couple days. After we drop Jules off, the guys insist that I spend the night at their house. But again, the way they say it gives me the feeling that it's more a statement and less of a question of if I'll spend the night.

When we get back to their place, Wolf races upstairs and comes back with a worn Broncos football jersey. My brow lifts questionably at the material in my hands but Wolf shrugs, his hands stuffed into the front pockets of his black jeans and shoulders almost hitting his ears.

"It was the first thing I grabbed," he says, sheepishly. I think it's cute.

I bring the jersey up to my face and inhale the unmistakable scent of Wolf.

It's earthy and kind of reminds me of the smell right after a rain storm.

"You can pick any bedroom," Jagger says, tipping his head toward the stairs. "Hunter has the biggest bed."

"There was no stopping you fuckers from getting the same size mattress!" Hunter defends, but there's a slight curve to his lips.

I wonder if he did it on purpose because he enjoys having all the guys sleep in his room. I don't have time to follow that train of thought because Kane wraps an arm around my shoulders and pulls me into his side, pressing a kiss to my head.

"Get some rest. We'll be back as soon as we can."

"What? You're leaving?" I ask them all, straightening up from leaning into Kane.

He shares a look with the other guys and then glances down at me smoothing a hand down the back of my head to my back. "We kinda left my dad without an explanation. We need to go apologize and finish the meeting."

Thinking it weird that they can't just call and apologize and try to meet in the morning, I brush it off and give each one of them a kiss on the cheek before heading upstairs to Hunter's room. The first thing I notice when I push open the door and step inside is that it's twice the size of Jagger's room. The second thing is that it's not at all decorated the way I pictured Hunter's bedroom to look. I was picturing dark walls, dark bedding. Just an overall gothic theme. But in reality, his bedroom is decorated in seas of off-white, blues and greens. It a shock until I realize that I don't really know that much about Hunter. He's always the quiet one. The one observing everything from a distance. He almost seems detached.

I peel out of my jeans and t-shirt, folding and placing them on one of the chairs in the corner. I unclip my bra and hide it in between my jeans and shirt before slipping into the football jersey Wolf gave me. I momentarily debate on taking off my underwear too but decide to leave them on for now and open the covers to crawl into the middle of Hunter's bed. It smells of him, and that combined with the smell of Wolf on the jersey is a heady combination. It's not long before I drift into a dreamless sleep, not even aware of the bodies that crawl in on either side of me a few hours later.

CHAPTER TWENTY-FOUR

HUNTER

ONCE WE'RE ALL piled back inside the Ranger Rover, I peel out of the driveway like a bat out of hell, squealing round corners and almost lifting the car off two wheels. I don't know what kind of game The Elders are playing at, but it ends now. Kane curses from the passenger seat beside me and runs a hand through the grown-out spikes on his head.

"Do you think they know?" The question is directed at all of us but he peers at me.

"Guaranteed if they sent Morgan," Wolf says from the back seat.

"Maybe she hasn't told them yet," Jagger weighs in from beside Wolf, but when I glance in the rearview mirror, I can tell that he doesn't believe that. If Morgan even so much as suspects something going on between us and Arlo, she wouldn't hesitate to tell The Elders. For fucks sake. If we had known who her roommate was then, we would've moved her out of that fucking apartment. Except, they're not living in the dorms and Arlo owns the fucking apartment. Fuck!

"There's no way they haven't know this whole time. She's been Arlo's roommate since the beginning of the semester," I say, half needing to speak my thoughts out loud and half needing the other guys to know where my train of thought is at.

"But how would they have known what she would mean to us? They couldn't." Jagger says.

"Unless," Kane starts, pulling at the new piercing addition to his bottom lip and staring out the passenger window.

"Unless?" Jagger prompts.

Kane sighs. "Unless her father isn't really dead." He repositions himself in his seat so he can look at me while also being able to look into the back seat. "We've always operated on the assumption that her father really did die thirteen years ago, but what if—"

"He faked his own death," Wolf jumps in, interrupting Kane.

"That still doesn't explain how The Elders would know about Arlo. Joseph died so that they *wouldn't* know about her. Seems counterproductive," Jagger adds and I have to agree with him.

Before we can argue the merits of why Arlo's father did or did not fake his own death, I pull the car into the driveway of the cabin. Before I have it fully in park, the others are already opening their doors and jumping out. I set the alarm and have to jog to catch up to them as they ascend the hill overlooking the cabin and the forest where many of our hunts have taken place. I hate this goddamn place. I wish we could burn the cabin and the forest to the ground and be done with it all.

As soon as we get to the top, we're greeted by three older men in perfectly pressed three-piece suits. Perfect disguises for the scum of the earth. Nobody will know who they're walking by. They've chosen the identities so that they can blend seamlessly into the hustle and bustle of the business district of Toronto. But here, they stand out like the headless horseman at a polo game. Morgan stands beside them to the left.

"Hello, boys," Morgan says just the same way she said it at the restaurant earlier.

Kane snarls and Wolf and I each clamp a hand on his shoulders to keep him in place. I don't know what purpose she serves in being here other than to piss us off but we need to ignore her. Without giving anything a way, I communicate that to the other guys.

"She must be wanting to become the fourth Elder," Jagger says.

I cock my head to the side and study her. The fourth Elder was Arlo's dad when he was still alive. Morgan might think that she has a chance at the position, but Jo was a hundred times as powerful as Morgan is. She's delusional if she thinks that they'll allow her to step into the role of the fourth.

"Maybe, but we're not here to discuss Morgan's future position," I reply and the guys give a subtle dip of their chins in acknowledgement. The movement isn't enough to draw the attention of Morgan or The Elders, but because we're so attuned to each other, we notice it.

"Well," James, the oldest, says, gliding a few paces in front of the rest. I barely stop myself from rolling my eyes at the show of superiority. "It looks like you four have been keeping a secret."

"A very big secret," Sean adds from behind him. Sean is the youngest of the four, well three now, but no less powerful. "Tell us, how exactly was Joseph able to cloak his daughter for so long without us knowing?"

"Your guess is as good as ours," I reply for all of us. It's not a lie.

We're not sure how either, but she must not have been cloaked from us, because we sensed her the moment she stepped foot on campus. Did her father know that would happen? Did he want us to find her before The Elders did? And if so, why? What role exactly does Arlo play in all this? Both Jagger and Kane reported that they began to get their gifts back after sleeping with her and without being summoned to a hunt. Is it really that easy? It can't be. But stranger things have happened.

Randall stays quiet where he's standing beside Sean. He's the one I'm most leery of. He's the observer of the group, like me. We see things others often overlook. We're the first to see the telltale signs of our enemy's weakness. Well, not today, Randall.

James hums, walking a circle around us. If he's trying to intimidate us, trying to find a weakness amongst the four of us. He won't find one. He hasn't found one in a hundred years, and he's not going to find one now. Charlotte Williams or no Charlotte Williams. Eventually he returns to the front and moves to stand back beside the other two Elders.

"Well then," James clasps his hands in front of him. "If you're as indifferent towards her as you all seem then you won't mind if we have a little fun with her. It's…" he takes a deep breath and tilts his face toward the night sky. When he exhales again and makes eye contact with each of us in turn, there's a menacing look behind his black eyes. "Been a while since we've been able to play with a prey ourselves."

"No," Kane barks. "Absolutely not."

I see the interest blare to life in the eyes of all the Elders and I inwardly curse Kane and his big mouth. If he hadn't just shown his hand like he did, we could've maybe gotten away with shipping her off somewhere until after their interest in her died down or at least until after Halloween. With it being just a couple weeks away we're too close to the veil between the two worlds being down. They're too powerful right now. But after Halloween, they'll be no more than puppies playing at a dog fight. James grins at Kane's outburst and floats closer, but to my surprise or shock, he doesn't stop in front of Kane. It's Wolf he stops in front of. Wolf doesn't realize James had moved until he diverts his gaze from Kane and faces forward again. He jumps when he realizes just how close the older man is. Well, older in human years. In reality, we're a few centuries older than them. Even though it doesn't fucking seem like it right now. I tighten my fist, digging my nails into my palm and clench my jaw. As soon as we get our gifts back, I'm putting these fuckers in the ground where they belong.

James grips Wolf's chin in his hand. He flinches from the strength behind James' grip.

"Tell me, Wolf, what does the girl mean to you?"

"With all due respect, you can go fuck yourself," he snarls, spitting in James' face. The act of defiance would've been funny if Wolf wasn't whimpering and forced to his knees by whatever one of the gifts James has chosen to use against him.

Having your own gift used against you is not a warm and bubbly feeling. It sucks. It sucks so fucking much. I actually believe that when our gifts are used against us, it hurts us ten times worse than anyone we could use them on.

"Wait," I call out to James before I can even think about what I'm about to do. "We're…" I pause and have to suck in a breath while ignoring the way my stomach rolls at the next words out of my mouth. "We were going to hunt her on Halloween."

That gets James' attention and he releases Wolf who crumples to the ground in a motionless heap. Thankfully, Jagger and Kane quickly move to his side to see if he's okay. Which means I now have James' full attention. Normally that would be a very bad thing, but in this case if it happens to save one of the men I love from pain, then I'll do anything.

"Really? Well, isn't that interesting?"

I swallow hard and keep my focus on James, and steel myself for this next bit. "She's just a plaything for us to pass the time. We were hoping that with your permission, we could celebrate this Halloween with a special hunt just for the four of us."

"Hunter, what the fuck are you doing?" Jagger's voice rings out, loud and clear, in my head along with the others but I ignore them. We all knew this was going to end one way or another.

CHAPTER TWENTY-FIVE

ARLO

HOT. SO HOT. That's the first thought I have as I'm waking up the next morning. I feel like I fell asleep in a sauna. I kick off the blankets, but immediately pause when someone grunts beside me. *Why is there someone in my bed?* Chuckles sound around the room as memories of last night begin to slowly seep back in and Hunter groans beside me, turning on his back.

"What the hell was that for?" He asks.

I paste on the most innocent look I can and smile at him. "I was hot. You all are like one giant furnace."

The bed dips and shifts behind me as someone rolls onto their side. A hard chest is pressed into my back as a very manly arm wraps around my waist and pulls me back.

"We can make you even hotter," Kane drawls, running the tip of his nose up the curve of my neck from my shoulder and nips my earlobe.

I shiver, arching my back and pressing my ass harder into the growing erection behind his boxers. Hunter squeezes my hip and then slides his hand up and under the jersey I slept in last night.

"I think it's time to get rid of this thing," he says, getting on to his knees and helping me sit up so that Kane can lift the jersey up and over my head.

As soon as the material clears my fingertips, Hunter's lips are mine. The kiss starts out gentle and exploratory, and as sweet as it is, it's not what I want right now. I grip the back of his neck and tilt my head to the side, deepening the kiss. Hunter groans. His tongue licking into my mouth. With my hand still around the nape of his neck, I fall backwards onto the bed and pull him down with me. At some point one of the other guys must have shoved the duvet off the bed because there's a nice breeze from the open window against my legs. Hunter rolls us so we're on our sides again and either Wolf or Kane move up behind me. I know it's one of those two because their leg hair brushes against the underside of mine and makes goosebumps pop up down my legs. Hunter groans in my mouth and when I manage to remove my lips from his and look over his shoulder, Jagger is plastered to his back with an arm over Hunter's waist. I follow the long line of his arm down between Hunter and me to where Jagger's hand is wrapped around his cock. *Fuck, that's hot.* I don't have as much time as I'd like to admire the sight in front of me because Jagger moves, allowing Hunter to roll onto his back, bringing me with him until I'm forced to straddle his waist.

My mouth waters when I get my first good look at the tattoo that wraps around his shoulder and stops just below one of his nipples. As Jagger leans in for his own kiss from Hunter, I trace one of the dark lines of Hunter's tattoo with my tongue. Starting at the one by his nipple and following it around and up to his shoulder. Grunts and groans sound to my right and I lift my eyes to see Kane swirl his tongue around the head of Wolf's cock before sucking the thick length into his mouth. My pussy clenches at the sight, and I have the sudden urge to know what Wolf tastes like on Kane's tongue. When Wolf's dick falls from Kane's lips with a pop, I lean over and grab a handful of the shirt Kane's still wearing and tug him to me, slamming my lips on his. He opens for me easily. Hunter's grip on my waist tightens and his hips lift off the bed. The motion making the length of his cock slide against the crotch of my panties.

As if someone is controlling my movement, I rise slightly on my knees and move my panties to the side. Hunter eyes me warily when I take the base of his cock in my other hand and position it at my entrance. He hisses and his eyes roll back in his head when I slide down his long cock until he's buried so deep inside me. I'm still craving Kane's mouth so I pull him back to me and kiss him while my hips rock back and forth over Hunter. I vaguely register the bed dipping in the back of my mind and my underwear being cut away from me, but between Kane's tongue down my throat and Hunter's cock driving in and out of my pussy, I'm lost to everything else. That is, until hands begin roaming over the globes of my ass and up my back where they increase slightly in pressure until I'm forced to let go of Kane's lips and lean down over Hunter. Another hand fists in my hair and forces my head to the side.

"I've been dying to taste those lips," Wolf says in a rough voice full of lust. His grip in my hair tightens to the point of pain, but I don't care. My eyes drop down to where his tongue is running along the seam of his lips and I lean in, wanting to chase it with my own.

My sexual experience before this was very limited. I wasn't a virgin or anything, but the boy I lost my virginity too definitely didn't know what he was doing. Hell, we both didn't. We were arguably too young to be doing any of the things we were, but I was young and dumb. I thought that because all my friends were doing it, I should be too. Once junior year started and I began focusing on my schooling more and more, I became less interested in sex and bush parties. Jagger was the first man I've slept with since I lost my virginity at fifteen. I never thought I would be here doing this. Having gone from no sex life in four years to sleeping with four guys at the same time.

Breaking the kiss, Wolf scrambles to his knees, working his fist up and down his impressive cock. He's not as long as Hunter but he's thicker and has a slight curve. A bead of pre-cum pearls at the head of his cock and I lick my lips.

Wolf chuckles, shuffling closer. "You want a taste?"

I nod, because fuck yes, I do. He brings the head of his cock closer to my lips and I don't hesitate, licking up the pre-cum and then closing my lips around the crown. Wolf groans, his fingers back in my hair and forces my head down further, making me take more of him.

Cool, wet fingers slide between my ass cheeks and circle my hole. I freeze and go still when a finger begins to slide in. Wolf pets my head and Hunter runs soothing hands up and down my sides and back.

"Relax, Little Lamb," Kane coos from behind me.

With Hunter offering little words of praise only loud enough for me to hear, I melt further into him. I wince a little when Kane adds a second finger but soon the pain gives away to something more pleasurable, and by the time the head of his cock is pushing at my hole, I'm distracted by the grunts and curses slipping from Wolf's mouth when he's forced to bend over me as Jagger fucks him from behind.

I lift off of Wolf's cock, and take his length in my fist, using the slight reprieve to suck in as much air as I can. Kane pushes me down even harder on Hunter as his picks up speed. I'm so full, it's bordering on painful but I don't want to stop this for the world. This whole thing feels right. Being connected to all my guys like this.

When did I start thinking of them as my guys?

I don't know who comes first but soon the room is filled with shouts and grunts. The fresh, early morning smell is replaced with sex and I wish we could all just ignore the responsibilities we have today so we can spend it in bed in a tangle of sweaty limbs and doing *that* again. I whimper when Kane slowly pulls out and then Hunter, hating how empty I feel.

Someone gathers me up in their arms and carries me to the huge ensuite bathroom, only lowering me back down to my feet when the water of the shower is warm enough. Jagger gathers me in his arms, my back to his front, and holds me while Wolf washes my body. I don't see Kane and Hunter in here with us so I assume they decided to shower elsewhere. Jagger must sense my deteriorating mood at not having Kane and Hunter in here with us because he grips my chin in his fingers and forces my head around until I'm looking at him.

"They're just changing the sheets, Little Lamb," he says then kisses me and I relax back into him.

After the shower, Jagger and Wolf switch places with Wolf holding me in his arms while Jagger dries me off with one of the fluffy towels in the glass cabinet on the far wall by the soaker tub. I'm happily sated and asleep again before Wolf carries me back to bed.

It's been two weeks since the morning after the guys brought me back to their house and left me to sleep in Hunter's bed while they went back to visit with Kane's father. When I woke up the next morning everything seemed fine. I woke up in a tangled mess of limbs and between Hunter and Kane with Wolf on the other side of Kane and Jagger on the other side of Hunter. We had a normal breakfast together and even made plans for the guys to join me and Jules at the club that night. But they didn't show up, and when I asked Jules if she had heard from Kane, she said that they had left town for the week and following weekend. I had tried to push the growing feeling something not being right down, but I just couldn't. Jules and I shared a cab back to her place after the club and I crashed on her couch. When I still couldn't sleep by the time five a.m. hit, I opened the group chat with the guys and asked them if everything was okay. Not one of them replied to my message, even though I could see that they had read it.

The next week was much of the same. I texted them but they would leave my messages only read. They arrived to Mac's class with less than ten seconds to spare before the lecture started and they were the first ones to leave. By Friday of the second week I was starting to feel like one of those chicks who just couldn't take a hint that the boy she was interested in just wasn't interested in her. I refused to believe that everything that happened between us over the last month meant nothing to any of them. So, in a last attempt to get some answers, I head to the gym after my last class. I don't know if Kane will be there yet or if he's even sticking to his normal schedule what with all four of them ignoring me for two weeks, but I have to try.

Sure enough, when I pull open the gym doors, Kane is already in the ring and it looks like he's been in there for a while. His back glistens with sweat and he's panting when he turns around at the sound of the door swinging shut. My heart sinks the minute he realizes it's me and he goes rigid. I haven't even stepped up close to the ring yet and I can see his jaw ticking from here. *What the hell did I do to piss them all off?*

"You shouldn't be in here," he says, his voice cold and not like the Kane I met in here a few weeks ago. "You need to stay away from us, Charlotte."

Heat creeps up my cheeks at remembering the dirty things we did in that ring and then again afterward when we were back at his place. I clear my throat and take a couple tentative steps forward.

"Please, Kane. Just tell me what I did wrong. I thought…" I choke on the sobs threatening to break loose and swallow them down. "I thought we had something good going."

He turns his back on me and drops his chin to his chest. I see his arms moving and I wonder if he's taking off the tape around his fists. "I can't help you, Charlotte. It would be best if you leave."

Charlotte. Not Arlo. Not Little Lamb. As stupid as the nickname was and as much as I didn't understand it, I miss it. It feels weird and cold not having Kane show that same care he did only a couple short weeks ago.

"Kane, please." Apparently, I'm not above begging. But seeing him like this. Feeling his cold indifference towards me is breaking me. I know what I need to do is turn around and walk back out that door and forget I ever heard the names Kane, Jagger, Hunter, and Wolf, but I can't. I just can't. It feels wrong to walk away from them. Like a part of my soul will never be the same without them now that I know what it's like to have them in my life. I don't want to give that up. I don't want to give *them* up. "Kane."

I know the moment he gives in to my pleading because his shoulders drop and he lets out a heavy breath. He still doesn't turn back around to face me but his voicc carries over loud and clear.

"Come to the cabin on Halloween."

"Okay. I'll let Jules know," I say, knowing she was looking for the ultimate Halloween party and their cabin would be the perfect place with its perfect mix of creepy and laid back.

"No," Kane says, standing up straighter but still not turning around. "Just you." Without another word, he jumps down from the ring on the other side and with his back still to me, strides off in the direction of what I'm guessing is the men's locker room.

The cabin and the driveway leading up to it are pitch black. I can't see anything, outside of the headlights of the Uber I had to call to bring me up here. When the car stops outside the cabin, I grab my overnight bag from the back and thank the driver before walking up to the front door. The driver doesn't even wait for me to be safely inside before backing down the driveway as fast as he drove up it. I ring the doorbell and wait. But nothing happens. I don't hear any noise or commotion on the other side of the door either. I pull out my phone and turn on the flashlight and then head around the side of the cabin toward the back. Tiki torches light the perimeter of the backyard and lead a path down to the woods. I shudder thinking about the last time I ventured in there and that brings up memories of the man who attacked me down the street from the guys' house.

"Little Lamb!" Kane hollers from where the guys are seated around a bonfire. They're all dressed in the same dark jeans and hoodie. "You came!"

I giggle, giving him a little wave, and drop my bag beside the log Jagger is sitting on across from Kane and sit down beside him. “Hey, babe,” he says, throwing an arm around my shoulders and drawing me into him. I melt against him when he plants a soft kiss on my forehead. *What is it about girls and forehead kisses?*

“You made it,” Hunter grins from directly across the fire with Wolf at his side.

“Wouldn’t miss it. I’ve missed you guys these past two weeks.”

Happy smiles and grins at seeing me, turn forced and suddenly none of them will look me in the eyes.

“So,” I say, trying to break the tension. “What’s the plan for tonight?”

Wolf chuckles, reaching down into the cooler beside him and pulling out a bottle of rum. “Now, we drink, roast hot dogs, and make as many s’mores as our hearts desire.”

I laugh, taking the bottle from Jagger when it comes its way to us. “I can toast to that,” I say, holding up the bottle in a mock salute before taking a shot straight from it.

I've lost track of how many times we've passed the bottle around, but it seems like it gets me to faster and faster every time. Or maybe it's become permanently attached to my hand and I haven't been passing it along like I should? I shrug. Oh well, their loss. My stomach feels all warm and my head is all soft and flowy, and I'm definitely drunk.

"Truth or dare?" Jagger nudges my arm and I almost go tumbling off the log. He laughs and catches me by my arm. "Shit. You're cut off, Little Lamb." He pries the bottle from my hand, but honestly, I'm happy to give it up. I don't remember rum going to my head this fast before.

"Ummmm, dare," I say, drawing the m out way more than necessary.

"We dare you to say yes," Hunter says. I squint at him through the orangey-red flames of the fire.

"Yes, to what?"

"Do you want to play a game?" One of them says, but I can't figure out which one. Their voices are all blurring together at this point. It's probably about time that I call it a night and go snuggle into Hunter's bed in the cabin.

"We'll even give you a head start." Someone else says.

Then I'm being hauled to my feet. Something is being shoved in my face but my vision is so blurry that it's hard to tell what it is. I blink once… twice… three times before the object becomes clear. Almost like a cold bucket of water is being dumped on my head, I'm instantly sober.

"You should've stayed away like we told you to."

"Jagger, what are you doing?" Each of my breaths come faster than the one before it as I look between the four men who are now standing in a line in front of me. All with the same cold, dead look on their faces and in their eyes. It's a look I've never seen on them before, but one that terrifies me. I start to back up, consciously aware that with every step back I take, I get closer to the forest and further away from the cabin.

"Run." This comes from Kane. With one last look at all of them, I heed his warning and turn tail, running into the dark forest.

Leaves and fallen branches crunch and break on the forest floor under running footsteps. Blood rushes in my ears and I quickly glance back, but I don't see anyone. It's dark. The sun having set hours ago already. The front of my sneaker gets caught on something and I flail as I hit the ground hard on my knees. Pain, hot and fast slashes across my cheek and knees, but I don't give it another thought. I can't. Quickly, I scramble up again, kicking off the other shoe and try to ignore the way sticks and stones dig into the bottoms of my feet with each quick step. The thin socks I threw on are doing nothing to protect them. I have to get out of here. I have to get back home and tell my mom that I love her. Loud cackles sound nearby and I pick up speed, veering off the hiking path. I refuse to die here. In this forest. By the hands of the men I thought I loved.

"Do you want to play a game?"

"We'll even give you a head start."

Their words from a few minutes ago echo through my head. Right before one of them shoved a gun in my face and told me to run. I've heard rumours that they could be monsters. I just never thought that I'd be the one running from them.

"Beware."

"Beware."

"Beware."

"Beware."

The word echoes around me like they've got me surrounded but I still can't see them in the dark.

"Beware of the dark for that's where the monsters lurk."

I scream and fall back on my butt in the dirt when someone lands in front of me in a crouch before he straightens to his full height. My heart lurches. I almost told them I loved them that morning we all woke up snuggled against each other in Hunter's bed. My stomach rolls and I want to be sick. I scramble backwards until I bump into something behind me.

"You ready to howl, baby?" I hear Wolf say behind me.

Hands grip my arms and yank me up until I'm standing. My arms are pulled back and a hand wraps around my throat while the figure in front of me steps closer. His face is covered by the hood of the black sweaters they all had on before the game began. When he's close enough for the light of the moon to highlight his features, his blue-green eyes look black in the dark. I don't recognize the Hunter I've come to know over the last month in them anymore.

"Please, Hunter. Please don't," I beg, tears now streaking down my cheeks. He continues advancing on me while two of the other guys hold me still from behind.

"I'm sorry, Little Lamb," Kane whispers close to my ear, his lips brushing against the shell with each word.

"Noooo!"

The last lingering flock of birds takes off from high tree branches. Their squawks echoing in the otherwise silent night, and then… nothing.

To be continued…

ACKNOWLEDGMENTS

Nicole, my ride or die. When I came to you with the idea for this duet you helped me run with it. Even when it meant early morning chats before work. Thank you for all your encouragement and talking me through the plot holes that came up.

Nikki, I love our brain storming sessions. You always seem to know what I'm about to suggest before I get the words out. Thank you for encouraging me to step out of my comfort zone with this series.

Sarah S. Thank you for agreeing to proofread for me at the last minute. You're a life saver.

My Alpha readers, Joy and Sarah D, you ladies are awesome. I don't think this book would've been written as fast as it had if it weren't for the two of you.

Thank you to all the readers. I realize that this duet is not something you'd usually expect from me, but I can't begin to tell you how much it means that you took a chance on it anyway. From the bottom of my heart, thank you.

ABOUT THE AUTHOR

A.J. Daniels is now writing as Andréa Joy

Andréa is a shark obsessed; beach loving girl forced to endure the long Canadian winters. When she's not writing, in a lecture at the local university, or at her big girl job, you can find her binge-watching true crime shows, *Bones*, *911 Lone Star*, or *Friends*. Coffee is her love language.

If you enjoyed *Cursed* please consider leaving a review on your favourite eBook retailer and Goodreads.

Sign up for my newsletter to get the most up to date information on new releases: https://bit.ly/2SQp8sk

Make sure to join my Facebook group as well: A.J.'s Naughty Angels

ALSO BY ANDRÉA JOY

The Fallen Duet

Cursed

Redeemed (Dec 15, 2020)

Famiglia Series

Dark Desire (Famiglia 1)

Dark Betrayal (Famiglia 2)

Deadly Intentions (Famiglia 2.5)

Dark Illusion (Famiglia 3)

Deadly Surrender (Famiglia 3.5)

A Famiglia Christmas

Bound To You (A Famiglia Novella)

Dark Obsession (Famiglia 4)

Twist Of Fate Series

Then There Was You (Twist of Fate 1)

CPSIA information can be obtained
at www.ICGtesting.com
Printed in the USA
LVHW100354010622
720210LV00005B/72

9 781999 241339